Had she been too hasty?

Conte Alessio's eyes narrowed, almost as if he read her thoughts. Then his mouth lifted up at one corner. She couldn't call it a smile. There was nothing warm or carefree about it. Nevertheless, she couldn't drag her gaze away from that hint of dark amusement.

She stood transfixed, wondering how sensible her plan to work here for three months really was.

"My temporary housekeeper?" he mused.

Gone was the gruff challenge. His voice was soft as velvet and dark with something she didn't recognize, an undercurrent that eddied around her suddenly wobbly knees. It made her wish, again, that she wore her housekeeping clothes, instead of a dripping wet swimsuit.

The conte kept his eyes on hers.

But for the first time in years, Charlotte felt out of her depth, unsettled by the unfamiliar coiling heat low in her pelvis.

And the uncanny suspicion he knew it.

"I'll see you in my study in thirty minutes."

His tone suggested her first day was going to be even more difficult than she'd feared.

Growing up near the beach, **Annie West** spent lots of time observing tall, burnished lifeguards—early research! Now she spends her days fantasizing about gorgeous men and their love lives. Annie has been a reader all her life. She also loves travel, long walks, good company and great food. You can contact her at annie@annie-west.com or via PO Box 1041, Warners Bay, NSW 2282, Australia.

Books by Annie West

Harlequin Presents

A Consequence Made in Greece
The Innocent's Protector in Paradise
One Night with Her Forgotten Husband
The Desert King Meets His Match
Reclaiming His Runaway Cinderella
Reunited by the Greek's Baby

Royal Scandals

Pregnant with His Majesty's Heir
Claiming His Virgin Princess

Visit the Author Profile page
at Harlequin.com for more titles.

Annie West

THE HOUSEKEEPER AND THE BROODING BILLIONAIRE

HARLEQUIN®
PRESENTS™

Recycling programs for this product may not exist in your area.

ISBN-13: 978-1-335-58440-3

The Housekeeper and the Brooding Billionaire

Harlequin Enterprises ULC
22 Adelaide St. West, 41st Floor
Toronto, Ontario M5H 4E3, Canada
www.Harlequin.com

Printed in U.S.A.

THE HOUSEKEEPER AND THE BROODING BILLIONAIRE

With special thanks to the lovely Franca Poli, who is always so supportive and ready to help with my queries.

This one is for Dottie Auletto, a good friend who always had such faith in my stories and who will be greatly missed.

CHAPTER ONE

HE STOOD BY the arched window, staring into the solid wall of mist that covered the lake. It would suit his mood if that grey pall stayed all day, locking the island in from the outside world, away from the rising sun.

This day didn't deserve light.

Nor do you.

Pain jabbed his ribs, piercing yet so familiar he almost welcomed it. Pain was now a permanent companion, a sign of life.

Alessio grunted with mirthless laughter. On days like this, life wasn't necessarily a positive.

He scraped his hand around his neck, easing taut muscles. He'd been awake all night, using the excuse of the auction in East Asia as an excuse to avoid bed and the sleepless hours he knew awaited him.

The staff in the Asian office were the best. All his employees were. They could run a high-profile fine art auction without his online supervision. Even an event as spectacular as the one they'd just concluded, where fortunes had changed hands to secure some of the most exquisite antiques, paintings and ceramics the market had seen in a decade.

It had been one of his company's most successful events. That was saying something since his family's auction house had been brokering the sale of precious items to the world's elite for two centuries.

Alessio should be jubilant. His staff were. His extended family would be when company dividends were paid.

Yet he'd felt no pleasure at the success of an event a year in the planning.

Not surprising. His life was as much a blank as the lake mist out there. No peaks of pleasure or even satisfaction. Not since that day three years ago. He worked harder than ever, relentlessly driving himself, because to take a break would allow too much time to reflect and feel.

He shoved his hands in his pockets. He'd never marked anniversaries, but today's date was seared into his soul. He'd done what he had to, kept going. So many people depended on him. Family, employees, locals who looked to the Conte Dal Lago for support as they had for hundreds of years.

But keeping going wasn't living. Not as he once had.

His mouth twisted. He'd made many mistakes. He refused to add self-pity to the list. Rolling his shoulders, he forced his mind to the emails waiting for him.

A shaft of early morning light broke the thinning mist and Alessio froze, heart stuttering to a momentary halt.

He blinked. He must be hallucinating. Lack of sleep was finally catching up with him.

Or is it guilt, playing tricks?

He didn't believe in ghosts, despite living in the *castello* where his family had been born and died for over five hundred years. But what other explanation could there be for the shadowy form that made his nape prickle and the hair on his scalp rise?

He leaned closer to the glass, but the image remained the same. Below the tower, on the island's only sandy beach, was a figure.

Not one of the locals heading across the lake at dawn on some business. Not a lost tourist pretending they didn't know the island was private and off-limits to all but invited guests. There *were* no invited guests these days.

Alessio blinked, telling himself the figure would disappear, a figment of his imagination conjured by the toxic mix of emotions this date engendered.

The mist swirled and the person disappeared. He was telling himself it had been illusion when there it was again. Not just a figure, but a woman, a young woman.

He heard the breath saw in his lungs, felt anguish sink razored talons into his belly as she walked out into the water. It rose to her slender thighs, then her waist, her fingertips sending ripples through the water.

Like in your nightmares.

Alessio grabbed the window frame for support. This wasn't real. She wasn't actually there. She couldn't be. She'd been gone for three years.

Three years today.

Still she kept walking, not pausing like any normal bather on encountering that first morning chill. Instead she paced steadily deeper into the still, dark water, mist curling behind her.

Alessio's head swam, pinpricks of light circling in his vision. The stonework around the window abraded his fingers as he clutched convulsively.

Was he going mad?

His aunt had threatened it would happen if he stayed immured here, but he'd brushed off her concern. There were reasons he wouldn't return to Rome or any of his old haunts. A penance to be paid.

Mad or not, Alessio refused to wait here, wondering. He turned and strode from his study, hurrying down the tower's ancient stone staircase, its steps hollowed from centuries of footsteps, and outside.

The cobblestones were damp from the mist, but spring sunshine was already piercing the fog. He felt its warmth on his face as he plunged towards the shore.

There was nothing. No evidence anyone had been here. Nor any sound. Unless…did he imagine the soft splash of water towards the end of the cove?

He headed to the promontory, every sense alert in the foggy stillness, but heard nothing over the ragged rush of his pulse. He continued to the pier. The few boats there were familiar. Nothing to indicate a stranger's presence.

It had been imagination. A phantom conjured by guilt, regret and too little sleep.

Yet Alessio was too unsettled to go back to his office. He took the narrow, cobbled street that circled the island, past familiar buildings, some empty and some tenanted by families who'd lived here almost as long as his own, most of them reliant on his family for work. They were a tight-knit community.

Not for the first time, he felt grateful for the way they'd closed ranks when tragedy had struck. The paparazzi printed unspeakable things about him, and society gossips were agog with speculation. But not a word had escaped from L'Isola del Drago about the events on which the world continued to speculate.

He was a lucky man to have such loyalty.

Alessio's mouth twisted. Lucky? In his people's loyalty and in business, definitely. Three years of complete dedication to the company had brought unheralded success. As for anything else…

There is no anything else.

He inhaled the scent of freshly baked bread and realised he'd already circumnavigated the small island, reaching the tiny bakery that kept the residents supplied with bread and baked goods.

He could call on Mario for an early morning chat over a cornetto pastry. It had been weeks since he'd looked in on the old man. But he couldn't face talking to anyone today, even someone who'd known him from the cradle.

Especially someone who knew him so well.

Alessio was striding towards the *castello* when the mist on the lake lifted and with it every hair on his body.

She was there.

The woman he'd seen earlier.

A rogue shaft of sunlight lit her from behind, turning her into a silhouette as she emerged from the green depths and waded towards the shore, shoulders back and hips undulating in a gait that was pure feminine allure.

Alessio's heart threatened to burst the confines of his ribs as he took her in. Face in shadow, wet hair slicked back and clinging to her skull. Slender arms. Narrow waist and flaring hips.

He must have made a sound. What, he couldn't imagine, for his larynx had frozen. But she stopped, head jerking towards him as if she'd been unaware of his presence.

For another devastating second the illusion held, his brain telling him it was Antonia, or her wraith.

Except this was no wraith. Nor a haunting memory. The gap in the mist widened, the shaft of sunlight opening further, gilding the young woman's arm and one pale, wet thigh, turning her from shadow into cream and gold and slick, living flesh.

Alessio's lungs burst into life as the breath he'd

held escaped and he dragged in oxygen so fast it slammed into his tight chest.

Of course it wasn't Antonia.

She'd been gone for three years. Nor had she possessed a sapphire-blue one-piece swimsuit. Antonia had preferred bikinis.

He blinked, taking in the sleek shape of the woman who'd stopped in knee-deep water, as if wondering if it were safe to come ashore.

He would have told her the place was cursed, warned her to go back to wherever she'd come from, except his throat had constricted so badly it felt wrapped in barbed wire.

So he stood, hands clenched at his sides, listening to his drumming pulse and staring.

The high-necked swimsuit should have been demure, except it clung to delectable curves and a slim waist. Dimly he thought of the Renaissance painting of Venus emerging from her bath that hung in the principal guest suite. But Venus lacked this woman's punch-to-the-belly sexiness. Even her pale bare shoulders, glistening in the first rays of the sun, looked sleekly inviting.

That, finally, freed him from stasis. This was no ghost but a flesh-and-blood woman.

It was confirmed by his body's abrupt, almost violent response, a rush of what he could only label masculine appreciation. Because he refused to be more brutally honest about that sudden surge of blood and testosterone.

Alessio widened his stance, locking his knees, enduring a sensation like the thawing of snow-numbed flesh, painful yet invigorating. It had been years since he'd experienced anything like this.

Had his physical responses been frozen along with his heart?

He strode forward, furious with this interloper who'd mystified and aroused him, drawing responses he'd never expected to feel again. Never wanted to feel again.

'You're trespassing. Go away.'

It emerged as a growl from his tight throat. So be it. He, more than most of his ancestors, deserved the ancient, whispered appellation, Dragon of the Lake.

Yet the woman moved closer, swinging her arms wide as she waded. Sunlight caught the rest of her now, revealing hair the colour of the old gold jewellery locked in the vault below the *castello*.

Alessio scowled. Didn't she understand Italian? He repeated himself in English.

Even then she didn't stop until she stood before him, ankle-deep in water.

'I understood the first time. But I'm not trespassing. I'm Charlotte Symonds.'

Then she smiled.

Charlotte kept her smile pinned on as she looked up into his sombre face. Years of practice with demanding guests came to her aid, even if a warning voice cried out that this man was unlike any challenging hotel guest she'd ever had.

He was in a league of his own.

She breathed deep, searching for the calm that would help her through this meeting, and saw his gaze flicker as her chest rose. Something flashed in his deep green eyes that sent a jolt of heat to her very core.

The hair at the back of her nape prickled at her unexpected response. She wasn't beautiful, but she'd encountered her share of male interest and had perfected the art of the deft brush-off.

At the moment she felt anything but deft. And for the first time in forever, her instinct wasn't to deliver a brush-off. That derailed both her smile and her confidence.

'I don't care who you are,' he growled. 'This is private property.'

He crossed his arms, his stance pure challenge, as if preparing to repel her physically if she tried to get past him.

The idea was ludicrous. His cheeks might look hollowed beneath those high, aristocratic cheekbones, but he was tall and powerfully built. When he stood like that, feet wide and crossed arms emphasising the width of his chest, he looked immoveable and impervious. Not a man she could tackle physically.

'What are you smiling at?'

Hastily she flattened her mouth. 'I'm not smiling. It must have been a trick of the light.' She reached out to shake hands. 'How do you do, Conte Alessio? I'm—'

'Not welcome here.'

That hard, beautiful face with its long, sharp planes and intriguing symmetry turned to stone.

Except for the pulse thudding at his temple. It proved he was flesh and blood. As did the dark shadowed jaw and shiny tangle of untamed black hair. The combination should have made him look like a scruffy pirate. And there *was* something piratical about him, the air of a man who'd break every rule without a second thought if it suited him. If it meant getting what he wanted. His expression told her he was used to getting exactly what he wanted.

Despite the chill air, a curl of heat low in her abdomen made Charlotte frown. As if she found such ruthlessness arousing, though she abhorred bossy men who expected to get their own way.

Instead of looking scruffy, the man before her looked…indomitable. Imposing. Intriguing.

Incredibly sexy.

Charlotte should have been prepared. But the old photos she'd seen—of him clean-shaven in a bespoke suit, the epitome of success, or impeccably casual and stylish boarding a private yacht—hadn't revealed his raw energy. The stark, grab-at-the-throat magnetism.

She swallowed hard, trying to snatch control of her thoughts.

'If you don't leave immediately, I'll personally see you off the premises.'

'That won't be necessary.' Charlotte stood taller, telling herself it didn't matter she was in a swimsuit instead of work clothes. 'I work here. I'm your temporary housekeeper.'

He didn't so much as blink. The scowl stayed firmly in place. The only change was the lift of one coal-black eyebrow in haughty disbelief.

Charlotte's lungs tightened. But she was used to sneers. Her father was an expert, though in his case it was closely followed by a barrage of furious bluster as he browbeat whoever had dared stand up to him.

She'd long ago refused to be cowed by her father's threats. Her new employer would learn that a mere raised eyebrow wouldn't deter her. She might be an employee, but she wouldn't be bullied.

'I arrived late yesterday. Anna was going to introduce me personally when you were available.' Because the Count was not, under any circumstances, to be bothered while working. 'But a call came from Rome in the middle of the night. She had to leave suddenly.'

His folded arms fell to his sides. 'Her daughter?'

She nodded. 'There's a complication with the pregnancy. She's in hospital.'

Charlotte searched for some softening in his

expression, but his features seemed to draw even tighter while his large hands flexed at his sides.

Yet she could have sworn she saw a shadow cross his face, as if from pain.

Perhaps he wasn't as unfeeling as rumour had it.

Or maybe you're imagining things.

She'd always tried to see the best in people, despite close acquaintance with her father's nasty ways.

He pulled a phone from his pocket, scowling, then turned on his heel, lifting the phone to his ear, striding away on long legs. Charlotte heard him say 'Anna,' and then a stream of words that was beyond her nascent understanding of Italian. Moments later he'd put the phone away, presumably having left a message for his housekeeper.

Demanding she return?

Or enquiring about her and her daughter?

Charlotte had no way of knowing. His expression was just the same, hard and forbidding.

The stories she'd read about Alessio, Conte Dal Lago, crowded her mind. He was head of one of Italy's oldest aristocratic families. Descended from robber barons and warriors who'd carved a fiefdom for themselves in the lakes and mountains of northern Italy, who had prospered and finally turned genteel. Yet their reputation for ferocity continued. According to one site, the Counts from the Lake, as their title translated, were renowned as being the most loyal friends and the most savage enemies.

She shivered and rubbed her hands up goose-pimpled arms.

When she'd read about his family, she'd been snug in her cosy suite in Switzerland. It had been easy to assume the reports were exaggerated as folklore always was.

But as the Count, or Conte in Italian, turned and fixed her with eyes the colour of the cold lake behind her, Charlotte recalled more recent stories. About this man. The recluse. The unfeeling, brutish Bluebeard. The cruel tyrant with blood on his hands. Speculation was rife about how he'd sequestered his beautiful socialite wife here, hinting she'd died of a broken heart, married to a pitiless tyrant.

Charlotte had dismissed that as media hype.

Had she been too hasty?

His eyes narrowed, almost as if he read her thoughts. Then his mouth lifted up at one corner. She couldn't call it a smile. There was nothing warm or carefree about it. Nevertheless, she couldn't drag her gaze away from that hint of dark amusement, if that's what it was.

She stood transfixed, wondering how sensible her plan to work here for three months really was.

'My temporary housekeeper?' he mused.

Gone was the gruff challenge. His voice was soft as velvet and dark with something she didn't recognise, an undercurrent that eddied around her suddenly wobbly knees. Whatever it was, it made her wish, again, that she wore her housekeeping clothes, instead of a wet swimsuit.

Not that he leered as some men did, who thought hotel staff might provide extra *personal* services. The Conte kept his eyes on hers.

But for the first time in years, Charlotte felt out of her depth. Unsettled by the unfamiliar coiling heat low in her pelvis.

And the uncanny suspicion he knew it.

'I'll see you in my study in thirty minutes.'

His tone suggested her first day was going to be even more difficult than she'd feared.

CHAPTER TWO

THIRTY MINUTES LATER, Charlotte tapped on the oak door of what she hoped was the study.

There'd been no time for a proper handover from Anna, and the map the housekeeper had left of the *castello* and its cluster of surrounding houses was sketchy. The idea had been for Charlotte to work with Anna for several days before the older woman left to be with her daughter for the birth of her first child. Instead, as Charlotte's arrival late yesterday was swiftly followed by the medical emergency in Rome, there'd been time to pass on only a few nuggets of information.

One. The Conte's privacy was paramount. Charlotte couldn't take photos on the island or discuss anything she learned about him, this place or anyone else here. As if the hefty penalties in the nondisclosure agreement she'd already signed hadn't made that absolutely clear.

Two. Visitors weren't allowed on the island without express permission. See rule one above.

If Charlotte had had any doubts on that score, her meeting with her employer had banished them.

Three. If the Conte was working in his study, he was never, under any circumstances other than a fatality, to be disturbed. No matter how long before he chose to emerge.

Again, see rule one above.

Four. If she couldn't make a perfect espresso, there was no point staying.

Charlotte's lips twisted in a tight smile. Apparently the demon count could be pacified with decent coffee. Though perhaps *pacified* was too much to ask. Given his mood earlier, she doubted a little arabica would make much difference.

What would it take to conjure a smile from those flinty features?

That, Charlotte Symonds, is none of your business.

She pushed her shoulders back, checked her still-damp hair was in its usual impeccable chignon, and rapped again.

'Avanti.'

She stepped forward, then halted on the threshold, her heart rising in her throat. Not because Conte Alessio was scowling, though this time his foul temper was directed at his phone rather than her.

It was the extraordinary room that stopped her in her tracks. It took up almost the whole of the massive round tower, with high windows on three sides through which morning light streamed. Beyond was an arresting view of steep-sided mountains falling down to gentler green slopes and the misty lake. It was like being in an eagle's eyrie.

The round walls were fitted with bookcases that must have been custom-made for the circular room.

Beneath the windows were deep padded window seats that would be perfect for curling up with a book or some embroidery.

Charlotte stepped inside, surveying the vast, extraordinary space. That first impression of cosiness altered as she took in the sleek modern cabinets near the door and the impressive array of computer monitors on the vast desk. Even the lounges grouped by a fireplace large enough to roast an ox had the look of modern design that married comfort with cutting-edge dynamism.

'Is that coffee I smell?' he asked.

He didn't even look up. His dark eyebrows were still angled in a V of irritation or concentration.

She'd give him the benefit of the doubt since it was clear he hadn't known of her arrival. Charlotte understood from Anna that she wouldn't see much of her employer. He hadn't interviewed her. Anna had done that after an initial interview by a formidable recruitment advisor, and the employment contract had come from a very superior legal firm in Rome.

Yet annoyance tickled her spine. She was used to providing an almost invisible service to wealthy guests, but surely he could acknowledge her as more than the bearer of coffee.

She walked, unhurried, around the desk and held out the tray she carried.

'Thank you,' he murmured, still looking at his screen. At least he had some manners. Charlotte recalled her father ignoring the staff on their estate, expecting them to anticipate his wishes and when they couldn't read his mind, blasting them with a violent tirade.

She saw the moment when Conte noticed the second small cup on the silver salver. He blinked as if it had never occurred to him that his housekeeper might appreciate an espresso after her early morning swim and his peremptory summons, leaving her no time for breakfast.

Or maybe you've gone too far, making a point.

At the small but ultra-exclusive Alpine hotel where she'd been head of housekeeping, she'd been treated as an equal by the manager. This was different, working for a titled aristocrat in his own home.

Yet Charlotte's mother had been an aristocrat, and Charlotte knew that a true gentleman treated his staff with consideration, not merely peremptory orders.

Why had *this* man's attitude irked her when she'd spent years placidly dealing with the most demanding guests? Even his gruff attitude was nothing in comparison with her father's furious rants. She had an unnerving suspicion she'd overreacted to his earlier dismissal of her, not as an employee but as a person.

Forest-green eyes locked on hers, probing. 'Please, take a seat.'

'Is there news from Anna?'

'Her daughter had an emergency caesarean overnight, but she's doing okay, and so is her baby daughter.' His mouth softened, and Charlotte sensed his relief. Perhaps his furrowed brow was a sign of focus rather than disgruntlement as he read the message. His next words seemed to confirm it. 'We arranged for them to go to a private facility with the best care in Rome, so hopefully there'll be no complications.'

We? Charlotte suspected *he'd* arranged it. She doubted Anna would be able to afford top doctors, nor would her daughter and son-in-law, who she'd said were saving every penny for a home.

Yet the Conte didn't have the smug look of a satisfied benefactor. There'd been unmistakeable tension in his tone earlier.

Face it, he's impossible to read. And it's not your job to try.

She moved towards a straight-backed chair before the desk, but the Conte gestured towards a pair of leather sofas. 'Over there.'

She took a seat, put the salver on a nearby table and sipped her coffee, eyelids half closing in appreciation at that first taste. When she swallowed, she looked across to find him sprawled opposite her, long legs stretched out, eyes narrowed. Had she pushed him too far? Surely he wasn't contemplating firing her before she'd started?

No, he was a man used to being waited on. He

wouldn't choose to fend for himself until he found someone to replace her. *She hoped.*

Charlotte sat back, crossing her legs. They felt cool, a reminder she'd had no time to pull on the tights she usually wore with her skirt and jacket as she raced to get ready and make his coffee.

As if he read her thoughts, he said, 'You don't dress like a housekeeper.'

The words emerged before she thought about them. 'You think I should wear a white frilly apron?'

'That's a French maid, not a housekeeper.'

His expression didn't change, yet she felt the blood rise in her cheeks and knew he was laughing at her. She couldn't believe it. She never let belittling or sexist remarks get to her.

Yet for once her usual calm deserted her. Her new employer sparked responses that were anything but professional, which was curious given she prided herself on her unflappability.

Had she bitten off more than she could chew, coming here?

'Is there a problem with my clothes?'

His gaze flickered over her straight skirt and down her legs. 'No problem. But Anna doesn't dress formally. You don't look ready for cleaning, more for a business meeting.'

Charlotte shrugged. 'In my previous position I had to look tidy for the guests, but I take my jacket off when I have to scrub anything.' She offered him a tiny smile. 'Sometimes I even wear trousers.'

His expression didn't soften. 'And what *was* your position?'

She frowned. It might have been Anna who'd interviewed her, but she'd assumed the Conte would review her decision. After all, he was a renowned recluse. Was he really so uninterested in who lived under his roof?

No, that wasn't right. That was exactly why he asked about her work now.

'I was head of housekeeping at a luxury Swiss hotel. I also filled in as manager for a short period.' It had been that experience which prompted her to look for a move. Charlotte was good at her job, but it was time for new challenges. She named the hotel and saw those expressive eyebrows rise in surprise. 'I can get my references.'

'That won't be necessary. Anna would have checked those.'

More confirmation that he hadn't been involved in choosing her. Yet now, it seemed, he had doubts.

Charlotte repressed a shiver of apprehension. This job was important to her. Most especially because one of the reasons she'd been offered her next position, a promotion to a famed Venetian *palazzo* hotel, was that she'd mentioned she was coming here to work as the Conte's temporary housekeeper. Her interviewers had been visibly impressed. The Conte Dal Lago had a reputation for accepting nothing but the finest in everything. Working for him was a sure stepping stone to future success.

And she was undermining herself, trying to score cheap points against him because he rubbed her the wrong way!

Get a grip, Charlotte. You can't afford to get the sack.

'I know the place. It's very well-regarded.' He paused. 'You seem young for such a position.'

Charlotte sat taller. 'I'm twenty-six in a few months. I've been working in the hotel industry for over eight years.'

This wasn't the first time people had underestimated her because of her age. But she was dedicated, determined and organised. Growing up helping her mother had taught her so much before she'd even begun her first job in a Swiss chalet hotel.

People had looked at her mother and seen glamour and privilege, the country estate and high society guests. Her mother had made it look easy as she managed the estate and its employees, ran her equestrian business and acted as society hostess. But behind the grace and calm had been hard work, excellent planning and social skills, plus the ability to handle any crisis. Charlotte had been her apprentice until the year she turned seventeen.

She swallowed, thrusting aside painful memories. She hadn't been home since the year her mother died.

The truth behind Charlotte's career success boiled down to one thing. *Desperation.*

Her career meant everything. It had saved her from her father's appalling plans and filled the void of all she'd lost. It gave her hope for a future built on *her* terms. Where *her* choices and *her* happiness mattered, and she wasn't a pawn in her father's endless quest for more influence and money.

Charlotte looked up to find that steady green gaze fixed on her. 'They haven't been happy years?'

Charlotte blinked, horrified that she'd been unguarded enough to reveal emotion. Blanking out her thoughts was something she'd mastered early as a defence against her father.

'On the contrary…' She made her smile easy. 'I loved Switzerland. I enjoyed my job and I met wonderful people. I've been very lucky.'

It was a matter of pride that the girl who'd left school with barely passable grades, the daughter her father saw as valueless because she'd never follow him into the world of high finance, had done so well. He'd deride her since she worked in the service industry, but it was honest work and she excelled at it.

'There's no need for the hard sell.'

This time it was Charlotte who raised her eyebrows. 'You don't believe me? It's true, I assure you.'

'Okay, tell me three things you liked about it. Off the top of your head. Don't stop to think.'

The Conte leaned forward, and she caught the

scent of cedar and something smoky, like incense. Instinctively she drew a deeper breath.

'I…'

'No thinking, just tell me, quick.' He snapped his fingers. 'Three reasons you liked it there.'

'The mountains,' she found herself saying.

'And?' He was in her space now, forcing her on. 'What else?'

'Doing a job well.'

'And?'

'I could be me there.'

Charlotte gasped as the words emerged. Her heart hammered high and hard as if she'd run up one of those mountains she loved so much. As if he'd probed too deep, making her reveal things that felt too personal. She put her cup down, barely resisting the urge to cross her arms protectively over her body.

'What do you mean, you could be you?'

Of course he'd locked onto that unguarded revelation.

Amazing how that confession felt so visceral. Even after all these years, it felt like prodding a bruise, thinking of the life and expectations she'd left behind in England. Of how she'd never measured up, no matter how she tried. Not that she had regrets. She loved her life.

'Ms Symonds?'

Charlotte met his stare, hiding resentment at the way he insisted on probing into her personal life.

If he had doubts about her ability to do this job, he had only to follow up her references.

Slowly she shrugged, allowing her mouth to curl in a small smile as if she were totally at ease. 'I told you I enjoyed the people, both the ones I worked with and the guests. And I made the most of the location. I enjoy hiking and skiing. I even did a little climbing.' She didn't bother to mention her other, sedentary pastimes. She couldn't imagine this man taking an interest in embroidery or cooking. 'The place suited me.'

Alessio surveyed the woman before him. She was hiding something. But was it something significant or something personal yet irrelevant to him?

He had no doubt she'd answered him truthfully. That brief moment of wide-eyed surprise had told its own story.

But Charlotte Symonds made him wary. He felt a jangle of the nerves, a frisson of warning, or perhaps awareness.

That stopped his musing. He hadn't been aware of any woman in that wholly male way since Antonia. He'd even noticed the fact his new employee didn't wear stockings. It didn't fit her conservative image, but maybe she'd run out of time. He'd been surprised when this poised woman, bearing excellent coffee, met his deadline.

She sat with her ankles demurely crossed but then shifted, crossing one leg over the other, and he couldn't help but imagine the slide of smooth bare skin against his own.

His belly clenched. A snaking chill crept through his veins, and the flesh tightened over his backbone.

He was *not* interested in this woman as anything other than an employee. His libido had been dead for years, and even if it weren't, he had only to think about the end of his marriage to kill his sex drive all over again.

Alessio's curiosity was prompted by self-interest. He had to know he could trust someone living under the same roof.

More fool him for not taking a hand in selecting her. He'd buried himself so deep in work he'd left that to Anna and his legal team. It was only today, faced with a stranger in his home, and one with an uncanny knack for unsettling him, that he faced the consequences of his determination to ignore the changes Anna's absence created.

'You understand no one else lives in the *castello*? It's just me and my housekeeper.'

Slowly she nodded, giving a good appearance of confidence, but he guessed from that flicker of her lashes that this was news.

Was it enough to make her turn tail and leave?

He almost wished she would. Something about Charlotte Symonds spelled trouble, though he couldn't put his finger on what. The discomfort he'd felt since he'd first seen her was instinct telling him life would be easier without her here.

Life? What life? According to Beatrice, you don't have a life. You just exist.

Only his Great-Aunt Beatrice, who'd known him from the cradle, taking an interest him while his parents were off enjoying themselves in Rome, Gstaad or the Caribbean, would dare say such a thing.

'Living quietly doesn't bother me,' said his new employee. 'In fact, it rather appeals.'

His eyebrows rose. 'You think looking after this place, looking after me, is an easy job?'

A husky laugh escaped, reaching out and curling hard around his innards, until she bit down on the sound and wiped the amusement from her face.

Alessio was stunned to feel regret. That laugh, warm and low—a woman's laugh, not a high-pitched giggle—sounded…attractive.

It had been years since he'd heard anything like it.

'Not at all. I researched the *castello* before I came. No one could call it easy, maintaining scores of rooms across four floors, all filled with enough precious antiques for several museums and galleries.'

She *had* done her homework. There wasn't much information online about the interior of the *castello*. It was his family's home, carefully guarded from prying eyes.

'Six floors,' he murmured, 'if you count the basement and dungeons.'

That punctured her assurance. Her eyes grew round. 'Dungeons?'

'Several of them, and a torture chamber.' He felt one corner of his mouth climb higher in an unfamiliar smile because the look on her face was priceless. Desperate poise vying with shock. 'Don't worry, it's not in use. It's been generations since my family used such violent methods. These days we get what we want in other ways.'

He paused, watching the muscles in her slender throat work as she swallowed.

She looked wary rather than scared, and he had no interest in terrifying her by sharing any of the creepier tales about the old place. But she needed to understand her work here, if she stayed, would be no sinecure.

He sat back, eyes holding hers. 'That's the family motto, you know. *I take what I want and I hold what I take.*'

Unaccountably an image flashed into his head, of this woman in one of the stone-lined underground rooms. Her blond hair was unbound, spilling around bare shoulders because instead of a neat skirt and jacket, she wore that clinging blue swimsuit. She was reaching towards him, arms outstretched, not in supplication but invitation.

Alessio's heart gave a sudden leap and he sat

back, rubbing a hand over gritty eyes. Even exhaustion didn't excuse such wayward imaginings.

'Don't worry.' His voice was gruff. 'There are maids who'll come in to help you. Plus carpenters, stonemasons and glaziers who live on the island and do maintenance here as needed. Most have jobs on the mainland as well. Anna oversees all maintenance work for the *castello* as well as domestic housekeeping, though if it's anything particularly significant or an item needing extra care, it's always done in consultation with me. Anna should have left the work roster.'

'I'll look for it,' she said quickly.

'That's the *castello*. Then there are my requirements.'

He had to respect her composure. She looked politely interested, back straight, chin up, her expression serene. ·

Alessio knew what they said about him. Some people, eager to show their sympathy, had painted him as a pathetic, heartbroken hermit after his wife's death. When he'd rebuffed their public attempts to offer sympathy, and thereby worm their way into his life, the stories had changed. Many regarded him as a cruel monster who'd forced his wife to drop out of society and kept her here, a virtual prisoner.

His gaze went to the family crest carved above the doorway. There was the winged beast, talons out, ready to seize whatever treasure took its fancy.

Sharply he turned his head. A thousand needle pricks tingled along his spine as Charlotte Symonds' blue gaze meshed with his.

'You have no qualms, working for me?'

'Should I?' She shook her head. 'You need to know I don't believe everything I read or hear. I've learned to judge people on their actions, not what the press says.'

Alessio was surprised she'd referred to the stories about him when most people were too scared to, and fascinated by that hard note in her voice that sounded older than her years. The sound of a woman who'd faced some harsh truths.

'Besides,' she continued, 'you had great references.'

Startled, he sat straighter. '*I* had great references?'

She nodded. Was that a tiny smile flirting at the corners of her mouth? It disappeared before it could settle, and he told himself he was glad. 'Anna clearly cares for you very much, and after putting me through one of the most thorough interviews of my career, I respect her judgement.'

'She gave me a reference? What did she say?'

There it was again, that ghost of amusement curving the edges of her mouth. It made her regular but rather ordinary features suddenly compelling. He found himself noticing the attractive shape of her pale pink lips, the intriguing way her eyes tilted at the corners with laughter. The change accentuated her cheekbones too, giving definition to her round face.

'That would be telling. I'm sure you understand that we housekeepers know how to keep confidences. But it was, on the whole, positive.'

For one astonished moment, Alessio felt a bark of laughter rise in his throat. It was so unprecedented his whole body stilled. Laughter belonged in another life.

'On the whole?' He raised one questioning eyebrow.

She nodded. Then, as the silence lengthened, she added, 'I was warned under no circumstances to approach you in the morning unless I came with excellent coffee.'

This time Alessio couldn't hold back. His laughter echoed around the room, the sound like a ghost from the long distant past.

That recognition instantly dimmed his humour. He was amazed he could laugh today of all days, but he refused to let the thought take root. If he'd paid more attention to the world outside himself, he wouldn't now be confronted with a temporary employee he wasn't sure he wanted in his home.

'Your lawyer was also reassuring.'

'It didn't occur to you that he was biased because I pay his fees? For that matter, Anna might not have been wholly truthful.'

The woman before him narrowed her eyes. 'I believe she's honest. Besides—' she paused '—one of my hotel guests vouched for you.'

Alessio frowned. So much for the confidentiality clause she'd had to sign before arriving.

It was unexpected and disturbing when she continued as if she'd read his mind. 'Don't worry, I didn't discuss the job or you. I mentioned that I was thinking of coming to work in this region, and Signor Lucchesi mentioned the *castello* and a major charity event you host here. He was full of praise for it and for you.'

She must be talking about the spring festival. It had been a tradition for generations, celebrating the fruitful seasons, and in more recent years, Alessio had hosted a grand ball, raising money for projects to improve the lives of people in the region. The sort of projects that often slipped through the cracks of government funding.

Anna had pestered him about reviving the celebrations this year, but he'd deferred giving a decision. It was easier to follow his policy of ignoring things he didn't want, knowing people would eventually give up bothering him. After all, he personally funded many local initiatives. He didn't need a festival to remind him of his obligations.

Yet you forgot about the arrival of your temporary housekeeper.

Not forgot so much as ignored it, not realising how much time had passed, thinking Anna's departure was still in the future. Though long-suffering

Anna had tried to shift his attention to domestic matters. He'd brought this situation on himself.

He met Charlotte Symonds' wary blue gaze and admitted she deserved better than the gruff welcome she'd received. Anna would have been ashamed of him.

'I'm afraid it hasn't been the most auspicious start for you.'

She blinked, and shock crossed her features before she smoothed them into a placid mask.

Had he been such an ogre that the tiniest hint of warmth surprised her?

Not just an ogre. You've been ungracious and arrogant, the creaky voice of his conscience whispered.

She might as well get used to the working conditions now as later, replied the ogre.

'I lost track of the dates,' he explained. That was anything but the truth. He'd been fixated on today's date for months. This sombre anniversary had consumed his thoughts, and he'd ignored anything peripheral. 'I'd planned to discuss Anna's replacement with her before now. I hadn't realised you were due to arrive so soon.'

Charlotte Symonds stared back, frowning. She didn't believe him. But like a perfect employee, she nodded, the sunlight through the window catching her gilded hair.

'I understand. It must have been a shock, seeing a stranger on your private island.'

Not as much of a shock as seeing her in the lake on the very anniversary of the day his wife had drowned there.

'Conte Alessio? Are you okay?'

She looked about to rise. And what? Put one slim hand on his brow? He could almost feel her touch, not only on his face but elsewhere.

His chilled body thawed and ached. He told himself pain always followed a thaw. But this ache low in his body was different, something he'd never expected to feel again.

Abruptly he lifted his chin, looking down his nose. 'Of course I'm okay.'

But Alessio didn't feel it. His thoughts frayed, and making conversation was difficult. Images of this woman emerging half-naked from the lake kept playing across his mind, merging with older, less pleasant pictures.

He couldn't remember when he'd last eaten. Yesterday? The day before? No wonder he wasn't handling this well. He'd gone too long without food or rest, working for days straight. These unexpected sensations had nothing to do with Charlotte Symonds but with the way he'd neglected his body's needs.

He looked at her and felt his groin grow heavy and tight as he considered those needs.

Ones beyond craving sleep and sustenance.

Something punched him hard in the gut. *Shame*.

He shot to his feet and strode to the desk. 'We'll continue this later.' His voice was a growl.

'But you haven't told me about *your* requirements.'

Her words stroked fire through his belly. A fire he doused with the chill of remembrance.

Alessio sank onto his desk chair, opening a computer screen, not allowing himself to look her way.

'Later, Ms Symonds. Settle in and find your way around the *castello*. We'll talk about my requirements later.'

CHAPTER THREE

LATER MEANT *MUCH* LATER.

Several times through the day, Charlotte went up the tower's curving staircase to his study. Each time the door was shut. She'd been warned never to interrupt the Conte at work, and his expression when he'd dismissed her this morning made it clear their discussion wasn't a priority.

He'd already been looking at his computer screen, eyes narrowed in concentration as if he'd forgotten her presence.

Was it business that put him in that tetchy mood? His deep green eyes had held a febrile glitter that spoke of something more than concentration.

Emotion, and deep emotion at that.

She'd glimpsed hints of it despite his aristocratic hauteur and his grouchiness, like a bear disturbed in its den. He didn't like dealing with a newcomer, but instinct told her there was more to it than that.

You're not being paid to understand him.

Yet no matter how busy she'd been during the day, her thoughts strayed back to that fierce, daunting man who'd ruffled her composure as no one had in years.

He had the arrogance and brute power of his robber baron ancestors. If she really had been an interloper, he'd probably have tossed her back into the water.

She'd felt his nearness as a physical force. The angry glide of his gaze creating friction on her bare flesh. The aura around him, like a force field, was palpable. The flick of one eyebrow, the flare of chiselled nostrils, igniting a rush of heat inside her.

It was inexplicable. In Switzerland, many guests had been fit and athletic, there for the skiing or climbing. But none had such an overtly physical presence.

If his stare had been sexual, it would have been easier. She could deal with unwanted attention. It came with the job, sadly. But the Conte hadn't leered. He wanted her gone. Even when he discovered who she was, it felt like he'd prefer it if she ran away and left him to his own devices.

Charlotte frowned as she grabbed a tray and cutlery.

Whatever the Conte did all day, it didn't seem to involve eating. She'd taken stock of the supplies in the huge pantry, and nothing had disappeared.

All day, as she explored the ancient building and talked to the maids who'd arrived to clean the grand reception rooms, she'd waited for his summons.

There'd been none.

Was he still deciding whether to employ her? Charlotte's breath snagged. She couldn't get the sack on her first day!

Nor could she wait endlessly for him to re-member her existence. She had to know where she stood.

She'd take him dinner, knock on the door and leave it there if necessary. But with luck he'd invite her in, and she'd at least have a chance to sched-ule a meeting.

Charlotte laid the tray, adding some of the scrump-tious bread the baker had delivered. At least *he'd* been friendly, and the maids too, if inquisitive. Their welcomes had gone a long way to restoring her faith that this *was* the wonderful opportunity she'd hoped.

Minutes later she arrived at the study to find it empty. On a hunch, she took the stairs up another floor to the Conte's private suite. She'd explored it earlier, changing towels, dusting, and noticing that his vast bed was already professionally made. As if he hadn't slept in it since the morning before, when presumably Anna had tidied the room.

Or maybe he's incredibly self-sufficient and neat. Maybe he prides himself on his hospital corners and smoothing every last crease from that gorgeous dark green-and-gold bedspread.

Charlotte snorted at the idea of the Conte eras-ing creases when he hadn't bothered shaving in days and his hair was a wild tangle.

Wild but indecently attractive.

Her fingers clenched on the tray's handles.

No, no, no! She never thought of clients like that. The door to his sitting room was open. She paused and cleared her throat. There was no growling response. 'Conte Alessio?'

Nothing. She pushed the door wide and stepped in. It was empty, but the door to the bedroom was ajar. Presumably he was in there.

Charlotte took a moment to survey the room. The vase of ferns and spring greenery she'd left earlier looked good. As did the order she'd brought to the art magazines she'd found spilling across the coffee table.

It wasn't that she needed those seconds to slow her quickened pulse before meeting the demon count again.

Of course not.

When he thought it through, he'd realise he needed her. She could enjoy the job's challenges, knowing she wouldn't have the embarrassing, potentially catastrophic task of explaining in Venice that she hadn't worked for him after all.

Charlotte set the tray down on a table near the window.

'If I'd wanted you, I would have asked for you,' the deep voice drawled, and she stiffened, almost dropping the meal.

The idea of that velvet-over-iron voice summoning her because he *wanted* her awoke a feminine yearning so profound it shocked her.

Firming her lips and ignoring the way her nipples thrust against her bra, Charlotte took her time straightening. He would *not* discompose her or make her apologise for doing her job.

Fleetingly she wondered if his attitude was a deliberate ploy to make her leave. But why?

'I did call out before coming in,' she said as she turned. Whatever she'd been going to say next disappeared into brain fog as she saw him.

Towel slung around his shoulders. Lustrous, damp hair tousled from being rubbed. Faded, low-slung jeans, undone at the top. Bare feet. Bare torso. Acres of taut olive-gold skin.

Charlotte took in the image in a second of awed admiration, because, despite the now-familiar scowl, he was, quite simply, the most beautiful man she'd ever seen.

Except beauty implied softness, and there was nothing soft about all the lean strength in that imposing V-shaped torso. Nothing soft except perhaps the dusting of dark hair that shadowed and accentuated the shape of his chest and narrowed to a tantalising hint of darkness arrowing down into snug denim.

Charlotte snapped her attention back to his face and kept it there. But it didn't help. Something about his particular style of masculinity was emblazoned on her brain. Even the low curve of abdominal muscle and hip bone seemed branded on her retinas.

She swallowed, her throat sandpaper-dry.

'Next time, don't come in unless you're asked.'

'Of course.' She almost added that it was good to have him spell out some of his expectations but knew he wouldn't appreciate the reminder of their overdue talk. 'Shall I take the food away?'

Alessio looked into that butter-wouldn't-melt expression and had to force his jaw to unlock. He didn't want to scare her, precisely, but her refusal to react as expected was unsettling. Why was she here when he'd told her to keep away?

Even more unsettling was that today, for the first time in ages, he was so aware of himself physically. Of sensations and hungers he'd long forgotten.

The food smelled wonderful, and his stomach was empty. 'Leave it, now you've brought it.'

He was being churlish. Anna would have stuck her hands on her hips and scolded him for bad manners. Yet this woman merely stood, unblinking in the face of his bad temper, calm and collected.

When he was anything but. He'd managed an hour's work after she left his study, because he didn't want to go to the kitchen for food in case she was there. He'd needed solitude.

Finally he'd stretched out on a sofa and shut his eyes, knowing if he did manage a fitful sleep, he'd be haunted by Antonia's sorrowful brown eyes and fragile beauty. Instead he'd slept the day away! And woken to the recollection of sparkling blue eyes and an unfamiliar, husky female voice.

Woken aroused too, for the first time in years.

Hence the bone-jarringly icy shower he'd just endured.

Because of this woman?

Impossible.

'I'll leave you to it,' she said, yet she didn't move. 'Shall we make a time to meet tomorrow for our discussion?'

So that was it. She wanted to know where she stood. She was as pushy as Anna. No wonder the older woman had hired her. She'd seen the similarities between them. Though Anna knew when pushing too far was counterproductive.

'We'll do it now.' He sighed. 'Give me a minute.' Then there'd be no more need to interact with this disquieting stranger.

When Alessio emerged from the bedroom, he was fully dressed. A place had been laid with fine bone china, polished silver and a linen napkin. A crystal goblet caught the light.

He wanted to say she was trying too hard. He was happy with simple meals. But to be fair, no one had told her his preferences.

Whose fault is that?

He took his place at the table and gestured for her to join him. A sensational aroma hit his nostrils from the steaming soup.

'Mario, the baker, brought a basket of fresh mushrooms. I assumed you like them.'

Alessio nodded, his mouth watering. But instead of sitting, she lifted a bottle for approval. 'May I?'

He recognised it as a vintage sherry. 'It was the first sherry I found. I hope that's okay.'

Alessio shrugged. It would take several lifetimes to empty the fine wines in the cellar. 'Sherry with mushroom soup?' It wasn't a wine he usually drank.

'Trust me,' she murmured as she poured a measure.

The wine glowed like autumn sunshine. He swirled it, admiring the colour, then the nose, then finally the taste. A complex flavour of nuts and dark honey exploded on his palate, warmth trickling down his throat and into his veins.

How long since he'd noticed what he ate and drank? He eyed the old bottle, telling himself it was because this was an exceptional wine, but knowing that was only part of the explanation.

Ignoring the conundrum he dipped his spoon and tasted the soup.

'My compliments. This is excellent.' He took another mouthful and another, suddenly realising he was ravenous. He broke off some bread. 'Sit and tell me about yourself. Why you want to work here.'

She took the seat opposite, her posture erect. 'As I told Anna—'

'Anna's not here. Just tell me what I need to know.'

He had faith in Anna, but reserved the right to

his own judgement. After all, it was his privacy being impinged on.

'I'm English, but I've worked most of my career in Switzerland. I began in ski chalets. I have experience in housekeeping, reception and management. I—'

'Why not work in Britain? Don't you miss family and friends?'

Alessio watched her eyes narrow and her brow furrow until that blank, professional expression returned. 'My mother's dead, and I'm not close to my father. I found good opportunities in Europe and took them because my career is important to me.'

What did that tell him? She didn't have strong ties to her family. She was focused on success. He had to admire that—it was something they shared.

Yet working here was an unusual choice. He couldn't shake the suspicion she was here for more than work. To pry and sell a behind-the-scenes exposé?

Yet she'd signed a nondisclosure agreement. He'd checked today and found the document from his lawyers.

'You see yourself managing a significant hotel? Is that your goal?'

She shrugged. 'I'd like to work for myself eventually.'

'Surely a job like this doesn't fit your career plan.'

'I didn't answer an ad. A friend recommended me to someone Anna knew.'

Alessio put down his spoon and took a slow sip of wine. A personal recommendation rather than the usual process? 'Is that how you get your jobs, personal recommendations?'

She wasn't a stunning beauty, but there was something about Charlotte Symonds that attracted male attention. Attracted even his, which until today, he'd thought impossible.

Had she won jobs through *personal favours*? The delicious flavours on his tongue turned sour.

He would have sworn his expression was unreadable, yet it seemed she'd read his thoughts. 'Not in the way you're thinking.'

Her chin tilted, and she regarded him as imperiously as his Great-Aunt Beatrice, the tyrant who terrified the younger generations of the Dal Lago family. No one else would dare look at him that way, yet he felt no anger. He'd take offence if someone implied such a thing about his success.

'You don't know what I'm thinking.'

'I take my work and reputation very seriously.' Those blue eyes fixed on his unwaveringly. 'I've won every job on merit. It's not surprising I receive personal recommendations when I do my job well. Surely you find the same in business, that those who excel are recommended?'

Alessio nodded. 'So why this position? It's not

an obvious stepping stone for a career in hotels. Plus it's only for a short time.'

She eased back in her seat. 'I need to practice my Italian. My next position is in Venice. And...'

'Go on.'

'And I was ready to move on to something new.' Still Alessio waited. There had to be more. Finally she shrugged, her gaze flicking away, then back again. 'You must know your reputation. Working for you, even for a few months, will be impressive on my resume.'

He'd long since ignored the outrageous stories told about him, yet he found he still had pride enough to be annoyed. 'Because surviving to tell the tale will prove how good you are? Because I'm such a monster?'

That's what some labelled him.

Her eyes rounded. 'No! Nothing like that.' She drew a deep breath that pressed her breasts against her crisp white blouse. 'I meant your reputation for insisting on the finest. Your auction house is renowned for quality, and so is your personal taste. You only employ the best experts.' She shook her head. 'I never meant...'

'It's all right, Ms Symonds. I understand.'

Only too well. He really had been mired in his own dark thoughts too long.

Maybe Beatrice was right, and isolation was skewing his perception. But not without reason. Too many people had tried to wheedle their way into his world via one excuse or the other. All wanting a piece of him. In the old days, it had been his money and influence or even his body. More recently there'd been a prurient interest in his suffering, in uncovering the salacious details of his marriage.

'Conte Alessio—'

He raised his hand. 'My apologies, Ms Symonds. It seems at least some of what they say about me is true. There's something particularly…ungracious about jumping to such a conclusion about you. I'm sorry. Maybe I've begun to live down to my reputation.'

It wasn't a welcome thought. He might be a recluse, but he wasn't a barbarian. Or he hadn't been.

'I suggest you go now,' he said. 'It's late, and I'm sure you've had a busy day.' She opened her mouth, he guessed to protest. 'Tomorrow morning we'll go through everything you need to know about the job.'

Finally she nodded and rose. 'I'll bring some more soup. If you're hungry, there's also—'

'No need.' His appetite had died with the realisation of his boorishness. 'This will be fine.'

'Very well.' Was that *concern* in her gaze? For *him*? The possibility scored what was left of his ego. 'I'll see you tomorrow morning.'

When she'd gone, Alessio finished the superb soup and crusty bread. He might have no appetite, but his years in hell had taught him he still needed fuel for his body.

Who'd have imagined he'd spend the anniversary of Antonia's death fixated not on the painful past but the present and the woman who'd interrupted his peace?

Charlotte Symonds was the first new face on this island in three years. A reminder of life beyond this place. Despite working seven days a week, and online discussions with staff and clients around the globe, the outside world had never impinged on him as it had today.

Now he felt…different. More aware. More alive.

As if this stranger had changed the dynamic and jolted him out of his stupor.

Or like an animal coming out of hibernation. There'd definitely been something bearish about his attitude when he'd confronted his new housekeeper. It was a wonder she hadn't left on the spot.

She had backbone.

And more. His fingers twitched as he thought of her breasts against that clinging blue swimsuit. The gentle arc of her hips down to slender legs.

Heat stirred in his belly. A heat that had nothing to do with the soup.

Alessio shot to his feet, too wired to sit. He needed a distraction from his new employee.

For he'd keep her on as his housekeeper. He owed her that since it appeared she'd come in good faith. But that didn't mean he had to fall headlong into the dangerous temptation she brought with her. The temptation to forget the lessons of guilt and responsibility and think simply like a man faced with an attractive woman.

More than attractive. She was fascinating with her uppity defiance mixed with calm competence. And there was something else about her, something he didn't yet understand, that set her apart.

Alessio planted his hand on the cool mullioned glass and surveyed the dark lake, its edges marked here and there by the sprinkle of lights from small towns.

Three months. She'd be gone before he knew it. Nothing would change. All he had to do was ensure she kept out of his way so he could concentrate on work.

Simple.

So why the disquiet? The sense that his peaceful life was wobbling on its foundations?

CHAPTER FOUR

CHARLOTTE POWERED THROUGH the water, the morning chill bringing her still-waking body to tingling life. She'd discovered cold swimming in the Alps, and it was better than coffee for energising her for a day's work.

Though, if she'd wanted, she could have lazed the days away. The Conte wasn't interested in her work, so long as she provided coffee and meals on time.

In the week since she'd served him dinner in his suite, she hadn't seen the man. Not once!

She seethed at how he'd avoided meeting her again, as if she were contagious. Even for a recluse, his deliberate avoidance felt like an insult.

On her second morning, she'd gone to the kitchen after dawn to discover a note in spiky black script on thick cream paper. The Conte had left a list of his expectations rather than meet her face-to-face.

He'd given times for his meals. Contact details for suppliers and a few other, sparse instructions. He'd ended with food preferences: none, and key requirement: privacy.

He was never in the small dining room when she served his meals, and she waited until she heard him leave before clearing away.

The Conte Dal Lago was unlike any employer or guest she'd known. It should have been easy to meet his demands and ignore him, yet perversely Charlotte was more than ever aware of her elusive employer. And, as if his lack of interest were a challenge, working harder than ever to make the *castello* shine and her hermit boss's meals delicious.

Charlotte heard him on the stairs and would stop, breath tight for reasons she couldn't identify. She'd enter a room and *know* he'd just left it, though she couldn't explain why. It was only later that she'd notice something had been moved, like books or those glossy art and antiques magazines.

Making his bed, she was always aware of the imprint of his head on the pillow and that distinctive hint of earthy woodiness and frankincense. The enticing scent was stronger in the bathroom, especially if it was still steamy from his shower. She'd find herself pausing to inhale, a fluttery sensation stirring inside.

Clearing his neatly folded clothes, she was sensitive to the fact he'd worn them. Occasionally she felt the warmth of his body on the fabric and caught that other faint scent, of healthy male, that made her stomach dip.

It was appalling, reacting so to a man who wanted nothing to do with her. Not only appalling but new.

She hadn't been so stupidly focused on a man since

high school, when an earnest science teacher had tried and failed to help her grapple with chemistry.

The Conte was no well-meaning young man. He was like a force of nature. Elemental. Harsh. With an inner darkness that should repel her.

Instead it fascinated her. Perhaps because, while proving himself to be every inch the brusque, demanding lord of the manor, he'd betrayed hints of deprecating self-awareness. He'd apologised for his assumptions about her. And when he'd laughed, the rich sound curling around her as amusement blazed in those extraordinary green eyes...

She bit her lip. This fixation had to stop. Yesterday she'd found herself in the great hall, staring at a painting of a dragon-like creature emerging from a lake. Presumably it was the fabled local monster she'd heard mentioned. But what had drawn her wasn't any legend but the fact the creature's scales were the exact deep green of the Conte's eyes.

That had tugged her closer, and she'd noticed another figure in the small painting. A blonde woman in a long dress. She faced the dragon with a surprisingly calm expression, given the hungry way it surveyed her.

A shiver had sped down Charlotte's spine. She'd felt an instant affinity with the golden-haired woman, facing down a terrifying beast. Especially as its sharp, devouring stare felt familiar. But in her unruly mind, her boss surveyed her with an entirely different type of hunger.

Charlotte set her teeth and turned for the shore, furious with herself. She didn't need his company, or for him to look at her the way a man watches an attractive woman. She didn't need anyone. It was a luxury having time to herself. She spent evenings nestled in her window seat, sewing and watching the sun set beyond the mountains, bathing the lake in peach and gold before the sky turned indigo.

She was putting her feet down to wade out onto the beach when movement behind her made her twist around.

There was a hiss, a powerful ripple and tug in the water that instantly made her think of the legendary monster.

Charlotte's eyes widened as, through the last patch of mist, a sleek form sped past the island.

Her heart thudded, then eased as she recognised the shape. Not a monstrous creature but a rowing scull, moving at speed. She saw a black hull and a tall figure and exhaled in relief.

That's how he stays so phenomenally fit.

She'd seen him half-dressed and knew he couldn't spend all his time at a desk.

He's got a rower's shoulders and powerful thighs. And that's none of your business, Charlotte Symonds.

Pushing back her shoulders and setting her jaw, she marched up the beach and grabbed her towel. She had things to achieve today, and that included cornering the man who'd done everything to avoid her.

The question was, which of them would find the meeting more challenging?

'Buongiorno.'

Alessio stopped midstride as a door opened and a warm, slightly husky voice slid through him. A pang of something sharp pierced his belly as light spilled into the dark corridor, revealing the trim figure of his housekeeper.

His pulse quickened. Because of the ambrosial smell of coffee and fresh baked pastries she carried.

Not for any other reason.

Yet he couldn't stop his gaze drifting from her shining old-gold hair down her slender frame.

'Good morning.' His voice was gruff.

'I saw you rowing and thought you might like coffee as soon as you came in. Shall I bring it up to your suite?'

'No need. I'll carry it myself.'

Her thoughtfulness pleased him, but he didn't want to encourage her. He'd been unsettled all week, unable to give work his usual total focus, mind straying too often to the stranger in his home.

The stranger who looked remarkably svelte in plain black trousers and a crisp white shirt. Even her severe hairstyle, scraped back in a bun, accentuated the purity of her features, the wide eyes, straight nose and cupid's bow mouth that was surely even more plush than he recalled.

Slamming a door on those thoughts, he reached for the tray, only to see her shake her head.

'I need to speak with you, so I might as well bring it.'

And have her in his rooms again? He didn't need that distraction.

All week her presence had curtailed his concentration. Everywhere he looked he saw reminders of her. From the meticulously plumped cushions to neat stacks of books and magazines that he'd left open and spilling across surfaces. Vases of foliage and flowers had appeared in all the rooms, even in the deep window ledge of the turret staircase. Not huge, ostentatious arrangements, but artfully simple concoctions that pleased the eye and made him feel grumpy with himself about resenting them. As for the luscious hint of vanilla and cinnamon on the air after she'd passed by...

He crossed his arms, belatedly feeling chilled as his body cooled from that workout. 'I'm busy this morning. What do you need to know?'

She blinked, and he realised her gaze was fixed not on his face, but on the ancient T-shirt that stuck to his sweaty chest. Slowly she lifted her head, her expression glassy, and his pulse revved.

Half-forgotten sensations stirred. Foremost was satisfaction, because there was no mistaking that look for anything other than feminine appreciation. The other was anticipation.

Once he'd have taken her interest as a green light for—

Alessio stiffened. Women had no place in his life, not even for short affairs. As for messing around with an employee... Absolutely not.

'It's the chapel,' she said finally, her voice thick in a way that made his blood beat slow and heavy. 'One of the stained-glass panels is broken. You said to speak to you about significant repairs, and I didn't want to have it fixed without consulting you. That glass looks very old.'

'It's medieval. One of the *castello*'s treasures.'

Alessio swallowed a sigh. So much for losing himself in work. He took the espresso from her tray, careful not to brush his hand against hers. Yet he couldn't avoid that light drift of enticing scent. Was it a commercial perfume, or had she been baking?

'Give me time to shower and dress,' he said through gritted teeth. 'I'll meet you in the chapel.'

Fifteen minutes later they stood below a high, arched window. Sunlight poured through, bringing a kaleidoscope of colour.

'It's such a shame,' she said, looking at the glass. 'It's beautiful.'

She hadn't met his eyes since he'd arrived.

Because she knew he'd read her earlier lascivious stare? The idea both pleased and annoyed him. Pleased because there was no room for a male-female relationship between them. Annoyed because, despite that, part of him, the dark, dangerous part, responded eagerly to the notion.

Alessio gritted his teeth. What madness had invaded his blood?

He wasn't pining for female company. He'd been content all this time. His eyes narrowed on her upturned face. She was unremarkable, pleasant but not stunning.

He yanked his gaze away. This wasn't about looks. There was something about Charlotte Symonds that teased him, hooked him and wouldn't give him peace. Something that, impossibly, had woken a vital part of him.

'It was my favourite window as a child. All those animals lined up ready to go onto the ark fascinated me.'

Blue eyes caught his, and heat shimmered in his belly.

'Really?' Her crooked smile was somehow enchanting. 'I have trouble imagining you as a little boy.' Her eyes widened. 'I'm sorry. I didn't mean to—'

'It's okay. I suspect I was always older than my years.'

As the only child of absentee parents with high expectations, he'd spent his time under the control of a series of strict tutors, working hard to become worthy of the proud Dal Lago name.

Stolen hours with Anna, Mario and other locals had never made up for a lack of parental love. Was it any wonder that when he was old enough to attract female adulation, he'd sought respite from the demands of family responsibility in hedonistic indulgence?

Alessio moved to the window. 'It must have been that storm a few weeks ago.' He swung around when he sensed the housekeeper's eyes on him, and a once-familiar frisson rippled down his backbone. Awareness. Sexual interest.

Instantly she turned to stare at the broken glazing.

Wise woman.

'There's a father and son team here on the island who can fix this.'

'Really? Surely it's very specialised work.'

'It is. There's no one I'd rather trust with this. Their family has been working glass for centuries. It was probably one of their ancestors who made this panel.' Pride warmed his voice. 'One thing we've managed to do here is support our artisans. Many are in demand internationally because of their specialist skills. My family values excellent craftsmanship, and we've done what we can to support it.'

'I read something about that,' she said, surprising him. 'There was an article about specialist goldsmiths here, trained in a scheme run by your company.'

Alessio shrugged. 'My family has collected rare and precious things for generations. We've made that our business, brokering the sale of valuable art and antiquities. As a result, we need access to the best artists and craftspeople when repairs are needed.'

Alessio didn't add that he would still sponsor that and other schemes even without the auction house. While he appreciated skilled work, it was equally important to ensure employment in the region. They were his people. He took seriously his family obligation to care for those around him. Supporting elite craftsmen was a single strand in the complex web of initiatives designed to keep the area prosperous.

'How did you notice the broken window?' The chapel was rarely used.

'I had a call from the priest in Florence about his visit, and I wanted to check everything was all right first. I'll bring in fresh flowers and—'

'Visit?' He frowned. 'I know nothing about a visit.'

Her expression grew guarded. 'He said he rang last week and spoke to the housekeeper. He was following up to check everything was okay for this weekend.'

Alessio was already shaking his head. 'Anna didn't mention it to me.' But maybe she'd had no time, given her sudden departure. 'No matter. Ring him and tell him it's impossible.'

'Why is that?'

Her voice was soft yet there was no mistaking an undercurrent of—was that criticism?

As if his housekeeper had a right to judge his decisions!

'I don't receive visitors.'

Assessing eyes met his, and Alessio felt both curiosity and something else in Charlotte Symonds' stare. Disapproval? Or could that be…pity? He stiffened.

'You don't have to receive them.'

'Them? I thought it was a priest?'

'He wants to bring a group. A *small* group to see the chapel, half a dozen. He spoke in glowing terms about the artwork here and—'

'No.'

'You needn't see them,' she continued as if he hadn't spoken. 'They'd come straight from the pier to the chapel and be gone in an hour. They wouldn't come into the *castello* itself.'

Alessio shook his head. 'It's not possible.'

'Very well. I'll…' But she stopped, brow furrowing. 'It would help to know why. I mean, clearly a visit is *possible*.' Something flashed in her eyes. Definitely disapproval. 'I understand select groups used to visit in the past.'

She paused as if waiting for him to explain himself.

Alessio drew himself up to his full height. The Conte Dal Lago didn't need to explain his motives, especially to a temporary employee.

'Surely you have so much, so many beautiful things, that you can afford to share a little?'

His head snapped back as if she'd slapped him. 'You think I'm a miser, hoarding this?'

The idea stunned him. His wide gesture encompassed the exquisite chapel with its rare artworks, glowing stained glass and sumptuous furnishings. It was a remarkable place.

But he hadn't been in here for years, not since Antonia's funeral. A shiver sucked the heat from his bones.

It was easy to fill that chill void with anger.

'I regularly lend treasures for display,' he bit out. 'Half the family jewels are in an exhibition in Rome. The tapestries are just back from being displayed in Paris, and several paintings are on loan to galleries and museums for study or display.'

Those grave eyes regarded him, filled now with puzzlement rather than disfavour. 'That's very generous of you.'

Now she pandered to his ego? That goaded Alessio. He didn't need her endorsement. He did it because it was the right thing to do. He felt a deep responsibility to care for and share his family's treasures.

For years he hadn't given a damn what anyone, relative, friend or stranger, thought of his actions. He'd cut himself off from people and their opinions. Now he found himself irked by an employee's assumptions. Not just irked but trying to prove himself!

His skin prickled under her stare. Did she think him greedy? Uncaring? Or maybe she believed the wild speculation about him, hiding away from the world.

Aren't you hiding? Beatrice thinks so.

As if his great-aunt or anyone else truly understood the situation.

'If it hurts you to have people around, of course you shouldn't do it.'

That serious, sympathetic gaze held his. *Sympathy. For him!* As if he were someone to be pitied instead of the Conte Dal Lago, wealthy and powerful, a man who supported and cared for thousands. Whose business success was lauded worldwide.

'If you tell me how to contact the glaziers, I'll organise the repairs, then ring the priest in Florence—'

'Wait.'

Alessio hadn't planned to interrupt but now heard the word, sharp and silencing, reverberate between them.

What harm could it do? When they came, he'd be in his office, working—

Hiding out, said his great-aunt's voice in his head.

He looked down at the woman before him and consciously unlocked his jaw. 'Confirm the visit.' Her eyes widened. 'But I want you with them at all times. They go straight from the boat to the chapel and back. An hour maximum.'

'Of course. I'll see to it all.'

Her gaze softened, her mouth curling at the corners. Then she turned as if to leave. Or to hide her satisfied smile?

Alessio marched beside her down the aisle, wondering why he'd agreed to this. It had been his decision, yet he felt he'd been outmanoeuvred.

Because he cared what Charlotte Symonds thought? Because he was sick of Beatrice's carping voice in his head? The pair deserved each other, judging and interfering.

They walked out of the chapel, and Charlotte was aware of how he reined in his long-legged stride to match hers. Of the swing of his hand just centimetres from hers and the high ridge of his shoulder at her eye height.

Her heart fluttered stupidly at being close to all that vibrant masculinity. She was still catching her breath after their confrontation when he returned from rowing.

Wearing shorts and a T-shirt that clung to his body, his powerful musculature had been front and centre. He might have a rower's shoulders, but those sculpted thighs were works of art in their own right.

A weak part of her had fallen in a fluttery heap.

It had been all she could do not to let his coffee cup rattle on the tray she clutched.

No wonder she'd avoided his eyes in the chapel.

Until anger and curiosity had made her confront him. Anger because he'd reminded her of her father, a man who hoarded wealth but without a generous bone in his body.

When Charlotte's mother died, he'd sacked many estate staff, people whose families had worked there for generations. He'd pushed them out of their homes, remodelling them into 'executive-style country houses' to sell for a tidy profit.

But what she'd seen in Alessio's eyes had made her think again.

Not Alessio. Conte Alessio to you!

His pain, the dark void of suffering glimpsed in an unguarded moment, had stunned her.

And made her thoughts skew to the gorgeous modern bedroom she'd found on the far side of the castle, complete with a huge ensuite wet room, and through an adjoining door, a nursery in sunny shades of yellow. Her heart had clenched as she stood in that bright room with its empty cot, knowing instinctively it had never been used.

It clenched again now.

How much had this man lost?

The press spoke about his wife. But was there more…?

'Not so quickly, Ms Symonds.'

His words stopped her as she turned towards the kitchen.

Charlotte pulled up, head swivelling towards him. There was no grief or weakness in that severe, aristocratic face. The Conte Dal Lago looked totally in control. More, the gleam in his moss-dark eyes hinted at something disturbingly like anticipation. That, coupled with his air of untamed masculinity, accentuated by his darkly stubbled chin and unruly hair, made tension dance across her nerves.

'Yes, sir?'

Frown lines appeared on his broad forehead as if he didn't like being called *sir*. But formality seemed appropriate.

Charlotte clasped her hands and waited. What he said next stunned her.

'I'd like your assistance. Let's discuss it over coffee.' He nodded in the direction of the kitchen and reached out to open the door at the same time she did.

Long fingers brushed hers, brushed and tangled. For that skimming touch sent a sizzle of shocking heat through her, making her hand curl instinctively so that instead of sliding free it caught his. Her breath hissed in but didn't fill her lungs. Her eyes rounded on the sight of long olive fingers locked with her paler ones.

Fire swept her features as she realised she was holding his hand. The moment was brief yet seemed to stretch forever. Trying to persuade her locked fingers to open. Trying to pretend her body hadn't gone into spasm at the merest touch. Trying to ignore the awareness that shot through her, settling like a glowing ember deep in her pelvis.

'Sorry.' It sounded like she spoke over grated glass. Felt like it too.

Charlotte dropped her hand, curling her fingers tight over the hypersensitive throb where they'd touched. She didn't look up, didn't want to read his expression, but watched those long fingers turn the knob and open the door.

This wasn't static electricity. It was more. Something connected to the disquiet she experienced whenever she was with the Conte. Or thinking about him. Or recognising that dark velvet voice as it wound through her dreams.

The door opened, and Charlotte shot into the kitchen, relieved to be in her own territory.

Yet it felt different now.

The vast space, a vaulted room that combined massive stainless-steel ovens and refrigerators, several pantries and an ancient fireplace big enough to roast a bullock, shrank in size when her employer entered. He didn't loom but sat in a chair at the enormous table. Yet his presence changed the atmosphere completely.

Or maybe that was embarrassment. She'd overreacted to a chance touch like some cloistered virgin.

Fiery trails still ran along her veins. What did that mean?

The air crackled, and Charlotte felt his scrutiny as she moved to brew fresh coffee. There was a clatter and she looked over her shoulder to find him piling fresh pastries on not one, but two plates.

The Conte met her stare with a raised eyebrow. 'It was early when you accosted me in the corridor. I'm assuming you haven't eaten breakfast either.'

Accosted? He made it sound like physical assault rather than a request for guidance. But she said nothing, too busy digesting the fact he not only wanted her assistance but planned to share a meal. What had happened to her reclusive employer?

'Don't scowl. You'll put me off my food.'

Given the voracious bite he'd taken out of a pastry, it was on the tip of her tongue to scoff, for he was clearly a man with a healthy appetite, much healthier, it seemed to her, than when she'd first arrived.

Which is none of your business.

Even if she'd been reluctantly worried about her unfathomable boss.

She focused on the coffee and calming her pulse rate.

'That's better,' he sighed, minutes later after his first sip. He was already halfway through a second pastry. Charlotte pushed some fresh fruit in front of him and a jar of heaven-scented honey that came from his own bees. She was rising, intending to cook some eggs, when he reached out.

He stopped short of touching, yet she felt the

phantom weight of long fingers on her wrist. The sizzle under her skin was familiar now. Did he feel it too? Is that why he'd stopped short?

'Sit, Charlotte. I want your attention.'

He had it. Especially when he called her Charlotte rather than Ms Symonds in that dark chocolate voice.

A shiver ripped through her, and her nipples peaked against her bra. Disconcerted, she reached for her coffee and hugged it close. Maybe she was succumbing to a fever.

'I'm listening.'

A quick look confirmed his haunted expression had disappeared. So too had the anticipation she'd seen lurking in his eyes. But she couldn't relax. The curl at the corners of his expressive mouth warned he was enjoying himself. Was he about to test her? Set an impossible task she had to perform or get the sack, because she'd had the temerity to question his motives?

What had she been thinking in the chapel? The client was always right. She'd learned that years ago. Why persist in questioning him?

Because she'd hated to think he was like her venal father.

'I have a special favour to ask, Charlotte.' His eyes locking with hers made her pulse slow to a ponderous beat. 'You don't mind if I call you Charlotte, do you?'

Was it his deep, smooth voice, or that musical lilt

of an accent that made her prosaic, old-fashioned name seem almost alluring?

'Please do.' To her relief, the words emerged crisp and clear. Unlike the rest of her, which seemed to be melting.

'Thank you.' He paused. 'What I'm about to ask doesn't fall within your duties. It's far more...personal than that.'

Charlotte told herself she imagined his emphasis on the word *personal*.

Yet she didn't imagine the satisfaction in his tone. Or the lambent heat in those stunning sea-green eyes, or the half-lidded expression of expectation as he sprawled back in his seat. It was the look of a confident man, fully expecting her to say yes to his request.

Her heart hammered as she considered what he might ask.

Charlotte recalled the man her father had wanted her to marry. She'd barely known him, but he'd had the same air of lazy self-assurance, of casual anticipation as he undid his bow tie and backed her into an empty room, telling her there'd be no engagement until he'd had a chance to 'try before buying'.

'I hope you don't mind bending the rules a little and providing a little extra service. I'd be very grateful.'

The Conte had caught her gawping at his muscle-packed body when he came in from rowing. Had he registered her response to his touch? The way her skin flamed and her breath seized from the casual brush of flesh on flesh? A man with his reputation knew when women were attracted. He'd been a renowned playboy before he settled down to marriage.

Did he think she was available on request?

CHAPTER FIVE

'DON'T LOOK SO WORRIED, Charlotte. I'm not asking you to slay a dragon or do anything morally questionable.'

He wasn't?

'I'd ask Anna, but I don't want to interrupt her in Rome.'

Charlotte sagged back in her chair, torn between relief and…was that disappointment? If this was something Anna could help with, he wasn't talking about physical intimacy.

She lifted her coffee cup to hide her burning cheeks.

Of course he wasn't going to ask you for sexual favours.

Look at him! He probably had women queuing from here to Naples, eager for his attention. He might be reclusive, but he was a fit, healthy man in his prime. Until his marriage, he'd dated a long line of gorgeous, talented women, and then married the most beautiful, most talented of them all. His little black book probably bulged with the numbers of amazing women.

He would never be interested in a housekeeper whose idea of a fun evening ran to a long bath, then watching a film or doing needlework, or preferably both at the same time. Whose own father had dismissed her as a domestic dormouse.

'Though, now I think about it, I suppose I *am* looking for a dragon tamer.'

His mouth curved infinitesimally higher, and she wondered, if he did that often enough, whether he'd actually smile. She recalled how his unexpected laughter the first day had cut through her professional reserve and tapped into a shockingly responsive part of her.

Light danced in those devilish green eyes.

Was that a dimple in one lean cheek? It was gone so fast she might have imagined it, yet she *knew* he was amused. It was there in the smug way he folded his arms over that broad chest and the almost-smile ghosting his lips.

The effect was devastating. If he ever really smiled at a woman, or, Lord help her, *with* her, the female in question would dissolve with delight.

Charlotte sat straight, pressing knees and ankles together and clasping her cup tightly, annoyed that she couldn't keep her thoughts in order.

'You've got me worried.' Though not as worried as she'd been, wondering if she could withstand a proposition from the only man who'd ever made her feel so sexually *aware*. 'Can you please explain?'

'It's quite simple, and I'm sure you'll be just the person to deal with it.'

'*It* being your dragon?'

'Figuratively speaking.' He shook his head, and Charlotte was intrigued to see his expression soften. 'I lost track of dates. It's my great-aunt's birthday soon, and I need an appropriate gift.' He rubbed the back of his neck. 'You seem like a people person.' At her questioning look, he shrugged. 'You were very concerned not to disappoint our visiting priest, whom you haven't even met.'

There was a hint of steel in his tone, reminding Charlotte that she'd pressed her case perilously far.

'I'm hoping you can find something to satisfy her.'

Charlotte was about to protest that she knew nothing about his great-aunt. But hadn't she done that sort of thing before? Chosen gifts for high-paying guests to take home? She'd even found the perfect eternity ring at short notice for a guest who'd forgotten his wedding anniversary.

This was no different. Except she sensed the Conte enjoyed the prospect of her failing.

She had no intention of failing. She needed this job, she was good at it, and she'd excel.

'Tell me about your aunt.'

'Great-Aunt Beatrice.' He paused. 'Eagle-eyed. Sharp-tongued. She doesn't suffer fools and has an opinion on everything, particularly the foibles of her relatives.' Including, Charlotte guessed, her great-nephew.

'What does she like?'

'Apart from telling everyone what to do? Travel. Gossip. Fine food and wine. Jewellery.'

'What did you give her for her last birthday?'

'A Renaissance gold ring with a flawless cabochon ruby.' He paused. 'She complained it didn't have a secret cavity for poison she could use to dispose of annoying time wasters.'

Charlotte stifled a giggle and was surprised to see amusement lighten his stern features. 'And the year before?'

'Ruby earrings.' At her raised eyebrows, he spread his hands. 'Red is her favourite colour.'

'But she doesn't want more jewellery?'

'No, that year she complained the rubies were too heavy on her ears.'

'She sounds like a woman of definite opinions.' Charlotte rather liked the sound of the old lady, but she didn't relax. This would be a tough challenge. 'What else does she enjoy?'

'Quaffing champagne with cronies and bemoaning the younger generation. You'd think her harmless, sitting with her needlework, until you realise she heard every salient point of every conversation and has an uncanny knack of dredging them up at the most inconvenient—'

'What sort of needlework?'

'Sorry?' The Conte stared, and Charlotte stifled a groan. She hadn't meant to interrupt, but it was the first real lead he'd given. 'I don't know. Decorative stuff. Embroidery. I remember she made a tapestry cushion cover too.' For the first time since they'd met, he looked unsure of himself.

'Cross-stitch?'

He spread his hands wide, shoulders lifting, and she repressed a smile at his cluelessness in this, at least.

'You've given me an idea. Give me a few days and I'll see what I can do.'

The prospect of solving his dilemma and proving herself capable gave Charlotte the fillip she needed. And helped banish the memory of her earlier bizarre reaction.

As if the *Conte* would ever be interested in *her*.

There was no mist this morning as he trod the lakeside path. Already spring was advancing. Alessio felt its warmth and something else, an expectancy, a vigour in his blood he hadn't known in what seemed forever.

Change was in the air. And in him? He felt different. Unsettled.

Yesterday he'd stood at his window, watching the visitors leave the chapel. Charlotte had waved them off, the sun burnishing her blond head, and he'd wanted, badly, to go down and bask in her warmth.

Even when she was annoyed with him, she was concerned about him, trying to feed him up or make him more comfortable. It was her job. Yet Alessio felt she actually cared about his well-being.

Sure! Enough to accuse you of being an ego-centric miser.

But maybe that's what he was, trying to make the world stop because he was too guilt-ridden to face it.

A sound made him halt, and there was the woman herself, leaving the bakery.

She looked alluring even in dark trousers and a white shirt. Her neat uniform couldn't conceal those curves or long, supple legs. But it was the way she walked, head up, shoulders back, as if ready to face anything, that drew his focus. A more imaginative man would say she had an inner strength that would see her through the toughest times. A woman who could vanquish dragons.

Alessio stifled a bitter laugh. That proved he should have nothing to do with her. According to local lore, he as the Count Dal Lago *was* the dragon of the lake, descended from a line of rapacious strongmen who'd plundered what they wanted—lands, riches, even women.

Which made it farcical that he'd timed his walk to coincide with her visit to Mario's bakery. So their meeting would appear accidental because he was too proud to send for her. But it wasn't mere curiosity about yesterday's chapel visit that brought him here. He wished it were so simple.

He wanted her.

He'd tried to pretend it wasn't true.

He'd told himself he was overtired. But it wasn't sleep he craved.

He'd only seen her half a dozen times, but there was no mistaking the attraction. It had been there from the first, snaking through his belly and disordering his thoughts.

After years wanting nothing more than solitude since he couldn't find oblivion, suddenly Alessio wanted so much.

He moved closer. Charlotte swung around. *And smiled.*

That blaze of welcome punched him in the chest. Alessio's lungs squeezed, pulse quickening as adrenaline shot through his bloodstream. His stride lengthened, greedy hands curling tight as he imagined reaching for her.

Then, in the blink of an eye, her smile faded, and she looked away. When their eyes met again, her expression was blank of everything but polite enquiry. She was the perfect housekeeper, no sign of the vibrant, welcoming woman whose smile had lit the fire smouldering in his belly.

A chill of understanding prickled his scalp.

'Conte Alessio. You're up early.'

'Just Alessio,' he ground out, unreasonably annoyed at her use of his title. Because it was a reminder of the barriers between them.

He'd let himself forget. As her employer, he had power over her, a power he could never abuse. He abhorred men who used their authority to coerce unwilling women.

Would Charlotte be unwilling? Had he imagined her eager grin? He'd believed he read interest, more than interest, in her eyes when she looked at him before today.

'I couldn't call you—'

'Of course you can.' He sounded grumpier than ever. But he *was* grumpy, and with good reason. 'Anna calls me by my first name.'

'It's not the same. She's known you for years.'

Alessio paused, acknowledging her point.

But an obstinate part of him refused to be ruled by caution. He couldn't have Charlotte in the way he craved, not only because he was her boss, but for so many reasons, including that he had just enough decency left not to want to taint her with his darkness.

Yet how he wanted…

Surely he could have *this* at least? The sound of his name on her lips. Not combined with the formality of a title, but said simply the way a woman would speak to a man? As if they were equals. Or lovers. As if they connected.

In the world's eyes, they weren't equals because he paid her wage. To some, his inherited title and wealth put him above her. But Alessio knew the truth. Such things didn't matter against the true soul of a man. As his soul was lost, he felt no superiority.

In fact, having her interact with him as an equal would be the closest he was likely to come to a blessing. She occupied a world he merely viewed from the outside. A bright, wholesome place he no longer felt he knew.

'Conte Alessio? Is everything all right?'

Charlotte moved closer, and he caught a drift of cinnamon and vanilla. She even smelled wholesome, though she attracted him like the most flagrant seductress.

Had years of solitude warped his perception? No. This woman with her unexpected combination of practicality, determination and sensuality drew him at a visceral level.

'Everything is fine. I was considering your comment. Shall we walk?' He glanced at the open door to the bakery and was glad when she fell into step. 'The fact is, Charlotte, I'm not used to sharing my home with strangers. We're a close-knit community here, even more so since my wife died.'

He paused, stunned. It was the first time he'd willingly mentioned the traumatic event that had so changed him. Even more surprising was the absence of crucifying pain that always accompanied that memory.

'I'm so sorry for your loss.'

Bright eyes met his, but Alessio saw only regret there, not prurient curiosity. More and more this woman seemed exactly what she appeared, hardworking, decent, capable and, he suspected, warm-hearted.

All the more reason to leave her alone.

As if! He might have enough shreds of decency not to pursue her. But he needed something for himself. Just a taste now and then of her generous warmth, even at a distance.

How the mighty had fallen! He'd once had the world, and any woman he wanted, at his feet. How shallow that seemed now.

'Thank you. The *castello* may be grand, and it's also my workplace, but above all it's my home, the place where I unwind.' In theory, at least. In reality, most of the time he felt wound too tight. 'It took a long time to convince Anna and the others on the island not to use my title, at least when we're alone. I would…appreciate it if you'd do the same. You'll be living here for several months, and it will be more comfortable for both of us.'

He slanted her a sideways look as they approached the *castello*. Her knotted brow warned she had misgivings, but she nodded. 'If that's how everyone here addresses you, then of course I will.'

'Excellent.' He held the door open for her. 'I have a little time before my first online meeting. I suggest we share those pastries with coffee while you update me on yesterday's chapel visit.'

He should have known better, he reflected as he leaned back in his chair, savouring his second coffee. He'd only permitted the visitors because Charlotte had prodded and queried and he'd wanted, for reasons he refused to identify, not to disappoint her.

He should have followed his instinct for privacy rather than pander to a woman. Yet even now he found himself warmed by the enthusiasm in her bright eyes.

'Let me get this clear. He not only wants to bring another party of visitors to the chapel, but you want to make an event of it?'

'Not a big event,' she hastened to assure him, placing a sugar-drenched pastry on his plate. This woman had all Anna's determination and even more wiles.

Dangerous, murmured a voice in his head.
Delectable.

Alessio grabbed the pastry and bit deep into buttery, sugared layers. He'd be twice his usual body weight and suffering from tooth decay if he kept using food as a distraction from Charlotte Symonds. 'Go on.'

'It would still be a small group, no more than a dozen. But they'd stay for an hour or so extra. The first group got into conversation with the glaziers removing the window. Did you know that as well as repairing old glass, they make stained-glass lamps and windows of their own design?' She met his eyes and smiled crookedly. 'Sorry, of course you do. But the point is, the visitors were fascinated and eager to buy.'

'So this is to be a buying trip? I don't see the value if it's just a dozen people.'

'A dozen influential people, all interested in fine art, some working in galleries. And it's not only the glass. When they heard about the gold-and silversmiths, the woodcarvers, jewellers and—'

'Enough.' Alessio raised his hand. 'I get the idea.'

Charlotte tilted her head as if doubting. 'I know one visit won't solve everyone's difficulties, but from what I hear, it's been tough for some of the artisans. Given the economic troubles recently, there have been fewer commissions.'

'So an opportunity to showcase their work to the right people is welcome,' he finished for her. It made sense. So much sense he should have thought of it himself.

He'd been too wrapped up in his own misery to do more than what was absolutely necessary. Why hadn't Anna or someone else raised this with him?

The answer was obvious. He'd given orders not to be disturbed, and his people had respected that. But instead of respecting them by paying attention to their needs, he'd wallowed in his private darkness. Sourness filled his mouth, and he grimaced.

'Truly, it won't disturb you. We can—'

'It's fine. It's a good idea.' It should have been his idea, if he'd been thinking straight. Guilt gnawed at his belly. What else had he missed?

'You agree?'

'No need to look so astonished,' he said gruffly. 'If it helps the island, it's good.' In fact, it might be worth considering a more organised event on a regular basis, something the locals could rely on.

Charlotte beamed, and Alessio realised he'd do a lot to win her approval. If he couldn't have the woman, he could at least have her smiles.

'I'm glad you think so. It would be a good opportunity for Mario too. He wants to try some new products to keep his great-nephew interested, but he wasn't sure the locals would take to them.'

'Great-nephew?' Alessio frowned.

'Mario mentioned him this morning. He got into trouble with some other teenagers in his hometown, and his parents sent him here for a break. Mario is trying to convince him to become an apprentice baker.'

Alessio sat back, fighting a scowl. Not at Charlotte's news but because it was she, an incomer, telling him. Time was when he'd have known about it straightaway, especially if Mario was looking to organise an apprenticeship.

Alessio hadn't stopped by the bakery for a few weeks. For that matter, he hadn't been in personal contact with a lot of the locals recently, relying increasingly on Anna to pass on important news.

His stomach hollowed. What sort of Conte was he? What sort of custodian or, for that matter, friend? He didn't just have a duty to these people. He liked them, was tied to them, cared about them. They'd been there for him through those lonely growing up years. And more recently, guarding his privacy.

What had he given in return?

Not enough. Not recently at any rate.

Alessio's chair screeched on the tiled floor as he shoved back from the table. 'That all sounds good. Meanwhile I need to—'

'Can you spare me a couple more minutes, please? It's about your aunt's gift.'

The perplexed look on Alessio's face was priceless. Charlotte had to stifle a smile.

'But it's blank.' He examined the package of fabric and coloured threads through its clear cover.

'That's the idea. Your great-aunt will sew it herself.'

She found herself staring at his handsome face as he studied the cross-stitch kit, a knot of concentration turning his features from imposing to breathtakingly attractive.

Her throat tightened. She couldn't explain her feelings for this man. Even when he'd made her anything but welcome, he'd fascinated rather than repelled her, attracted her when he should have been no more than a difficult client. Today he'd shown another side of his personality. He'd been genuinely concerned about his community. Far from blustering about protecting his privacy, he'd readily agreed to her plan.

Now his concentration on the gift and his puzzlement made him look endearing.

Abruptly he raised his head, and Charlotte's breath caught as their eyes met and fire raced through her veins.

Endearing? The man should come with a health warning. He looked away almost instantly, but that moment of connection reinforced the fact that she was out of her depth with him.

'If I could show you?'

She took the package, careful not to touch his hand.

'A friend designs these to order. As a special favour she created this in record time. Fortunately the express delivery was even quicker than I expected.'

Charlotte was babbling, her fingers all thumbs as she wrestled to open the plastic. That moment of searing intensity, when she'd met Alessio's green eyes, had rattled her. Even though she knew she'd imagined something more than curiosity in his stare.

At last she found the design sheet and held it out to him.

He said, 'It's the *castello*.' He shifted his chair closer to hers, angling his head to see the sheet better, lifting his hand to trace the design. 'And the village, and the mountains beyond the lake. But how?'

'Simple. I took some photos and sent them to her. My friend specialises in making cross-stitch designs of real locations. Though this one was a bit more work than usual, especially given the short time frame.'

He nodded, his focus still on the design. 'I'll compensate her for her time. This is remarkable.'

'I'm glad you like it. All your aunt has to do is follow the design to create an image of the *castello* on its island.'

She'd gone out on a limb, ordering this without consultation, but she'd had to act quickly to have it done in time. If he hadn't liked it, Charlotte would have kept it to do herself, a memento of her stay.

Charlotte frowned, feeling an unexpected pang of regret at the idea of moving on.

'It's brilliant. Beatrice will adore it. Thank you, Charlotte. This is the sort of personal, thoughtful gift I'd hoped for.'

He lifted his head and smiled.

All thoughts of the future and leaving disintegrated.

She'd been right.

When the Conte Dal Lago smiled at a woman—*really* smiled—she melted into a puddle of pure longing.

Nothing had prepared Charlotte for this. Not her clear-eyed understanding of humanity's foibles developed over years working in hotels, nor her experience warding off entitled men.

Every strength she'd taken for granted, every defence she'd carefully built, crumbled as she returned that blazing smile.

She was in so much trouble.

CHAPTER SIX

CHARLOTTE HUMMED AS she dusted the top shelf of the towering bookcase. Despite her misgivings, things were going well.

For 'misgivings' read 'a profound weakness for her boss.'

Her breath snagged for a second, but she ignored that, reaching further along the shelf and humming louder.

So he was attractive. Deeply attractive.

What woman wouldn't feel a little flutter inside when he smiled at her? There was no harm in it, as long as she remained professional. It wasn't as if he were pursuing her. Far from it.

Their relationship had improved enormously, but it was still a *working* relationship.

Alessio seemed to trust her, unbending more and proving himself to be a man she could like. That didn't sound like much, but given some of the men she'd known, it was high praise. He respected her, regularly thanked her for her work and since their discussion a couple of weeks ago, had been out in the village more. She'd seen him talking with locals, and he'd taken over plans for the next chapel visit.

Charlotte put back the book she held and, grabbing the shelf, pulled herself on the tall library ladder further along the built-in bookcase. She smiled. This sliding ladder reminded her of her mother's precious library at home, the one her father had cleared out when she died.

The ladder stopped short of the end. Charlotte jiggled her weight, trying to shift it but it wouldn't budge. There must be a problem with the track. She could climb all the way down and try to fix it or lean just a little further to reach the end of the shelf.

Time was short. She'd promised herself she'd finish the top shelf before getting Alessio's lunch.

Leaning sideways, she reached for the last books. But as she stretched out and up, the ladder suddenly shifted in the opposite direction. She clutched for safety. A heavy book knocked her forehead and she winced. Then came an almighty thud as it tumbled to the floor.

Charlotte didn't look down to see the damage. She was too busy holding on. The bookcases at this double-storeyed end of the library were magnificent when viewed from the ground but too far to fall. Perspiration prickled the back of her neck, and her arms were rigid as she fought panic. She was stretched at an ungainly angle, but as soon as she caught her breath, she'd pull the ladder back.

Except it wouldn't budge.

She was just getting really worried when the ladder moved again. Not another jerky slide but a rhythmic vibration.

Seconds later heat surrounded her. A living heat.

'Let go of the bookcase, Charlotte. I've got you.'

She felt Alessio's warm breath riffle her hair, the brush of his big frame behind her, and felt relief that he was here.

Yet she couldn't unlock her fingers.

'Trust me, Charlotte.'

On the words, gentle fingers covered her hand, prising it loose from the woodwork. Her heart galloped as she realised she wasn't hanging on to the stability of the bookcase any longer, but then Alessio's hand folded around hers, pulling it back and curling it around the ladder.

'Thank you. I'm okay now.' And she was. She was perfectly capable of climbing down the ladder even if her knees trembled.

'Of course.' His chest brushed her back as he spoke. and now she was aware of his arms around her, grasping the ladder on either side. It was… comforting to have him there. 'But we'll descend together, just to be safe. Ready?'

'More than ready. I can't wait to get down and have a cup of tea.' Her words belied her unsteadiness, but did he hear the wobble in her voice?

'Take a step down, Charlotte.' He moved lower, and she hurried to follow him, surprised at how much she disliked the idea of being left behind.

They descended like that all the way to the marble floor, one step at a time, his arms encircling her. But when they reached the bottom, to her horror, Charlotte couldn't pry her fingers from the ladder.

'I'm sorry about the book. I'll pay for any damage.' Which could be expensive if it was rare.

'Out of the question.' His voice was sharp. 'It's my fault for not warning you about the ladder. Anna mentioned a problem with it, but it slipped my mind.' He paused. 'Are you going to let go now?'

She laughed, the sound brittle. 'In a second, when I persuade my fingers to work again. It's silly. I'm not afraid of heights, but...'

As she watched, Alessio reached around her, covering her hands with his and gently pulling them free. His voice soothed. 'You've had a shock. We both have. If you'd fallen...' His deep voice turned to gravel.

His hands left hers, and she was surprised at how bereft she felt. Until the world tilted and she found herself, for the first time in her life, held off the ground in a man's embrace.

Stunned, she looked up past a firm, familiar jaw with its dusting of roguish dark stubble to piercing eyes the colour of deep water. Except deep water was cool, and Alessio's eyes blazed fire.

Her heart leapt at what she thought she saw there. Not the disinterested look of a stranger. Nor annoyance at the potential damage to his precious book. Alessio's stare was intent, charged. Devouring.

Charlotte shivered, not with weakness or dismay

but excitement. She closed her fingers tight against the temptation to reach up and stroke his hard jaw. To slide her hand higher, into that lustrous black hair. To clutch his skull and pull his head down.

She snapped her eyes shut, willing the crazy thoughts away. Yet without vision, she was more conscious of his tall frame against her. Those strong arms supporting her. The rise of his chest. The cushion of soft cotton and solid muscle against her cheek. The heady scent of clean male skin just a breath away.

Too soon, or not soon enough, he lowered her to a chair. Charlotte stiffened, eyes opening and hands lifting instinctively as if to keep him close. One grazed his jawline, the other catching his hand.

Energy pulsed between them. A quickening that she felt deep within. For a second their fingers clung, and in that moment, it felt perfectly right. As if they'd touched that way a thousand times.

Alessio's pupils widened, darkening his eyes, and she leaned closer. His fingers squeezed hers, and she *knew* he was about to lean in and kiss her.

His gaze dropped to her lips, parted in readiness. The air thickened.

Then his hands slid free and he moved back, straightening to his full height.

'You're all right now. No harm done.'

He stood less than a metre away, yet the distance between them was immense and unbreachable.

A lump of ice settled in her middle.

The man doesn't want to kiss you. He can't get away fast enough.

Embarrassment flooded her, heat roaring up into her cheeks. 'I'm sorry. I—'

'There's nothing to be sorry about. It was an accident, and if anything, my fault. I'll have the ladder fixed straight away.'

He was deliberately misunderstanding, letting her save face by pretending to think she was talking about the trouble on the ladder instead of how she'd grabbed him.

Charlotte was grateful, of course she was, but the idea of him pitying her futile attraction ripped a hole through her self-possession. Fortunately years of practice at appearing unmoved in the face of her father's tirades and putdowns came to her rescue.

She rose, only slightly unsteady, and pinned on her professional smile. 'Thank you, Alessio.' Her throat constricted on his name. 'I'll leave you to check the book. You know far more about it and what repairs might be necessary. I need to go and see about lunch.'

'Charlotte...'

Already she was walking to the door. 'But I *will* pay for any damage.' Then, mercifully, she was out in the corridor and hurrying back to the staff section of the *castello* where she belonged.

CHAPTER SEVEN

Alessio swore under his breath. Then swore aloud.

It was no good. He couldn't settle. For the last three days, since that incident in the library, he and Charlotte had both kept their distance, yet his concentration was shot.

A chill frosted his bones. That *incident* could have ended in serious injury if she'd fallen onto unforgiving marble.

It would have been his fault. Anna had mentioned a problem with the antique ladder, and Alessio had said he'd inspect it himself. Then forgotten.

What if Charlotte had fallen and cracked her skull?

Another woman's life on his conscience.

Though it hadn't come to that, he'd still hurt her. The pain in her dazed eyes when he'd pulled back from her...

She'd needed comfort and reassurance, and he'd been too scared of the need roaring within him to give it to her. Scared that instead of offering comfort, he'd take what he needed so badly.

Each night he was haunted, no longer by thoughts of his drowned wife, but his housekeeper. That felt like a betrayal of Antonia's memory.

In his dreams, Charlotte's earnest eyes fixed on him as she reached out, and he didn't hold back. In those fevered imaginings, gentle caresses turned to animal lust, fervent demands and desperate orgasms.

Alessio scrubbed a hand around the back of his neck, feeling the tension that grew daily.

It was unreasonable to blame Charlotte. The problem was his obsession. Yet right now, Alessio would happily dump some of the guilt on her slim shoulders.

What the hell was she doing downstairs? Muffled sounds distracted him from important business. No matter that he kept his study door ajar hoping to catch a glimpse of her. He'd heard voices. A male voice too, not just the maids chatting as they worked.

She must have brought someone in to assist with a specialist job. Not the library ladder. He'd fixed that personally the night of her almost-fall.

Alessio shoved the chair back from his desk and stalked to the door. There it was again, a male voice. Then, unmistakeably, Charlotte's laugh.

Suddenly it felt like a savage, sharp-toothed animal gnawed on his gut.

If he didn't know better, he'd put it down to dog-in-the-manger possessiveness. Jealousy that Charlotte shared her carefree laugh with another man instead of him.

That was impossible. Alessio had never been jealous about a woman. He'd had his share of lovers, and his relationships had been easy, never fraught with emotion. Even with his beautiful wife, there'd been no question of jealousy. They'd shared complete trust.

What he felt now couldn't be possessiveness. Yet he couldn't think of any other explanation.

Alessio took the stairs two at a time.

He found them in the vast gilded ballroom. One of the enormous antique Venetian glass chandeliers that lined the centre of the room had been lowered to just above the parquet floor. A vast trestle table had been set up nearby, where three maids were carefully cleaning individual glass drops. Ennio, the specialist who cared for the *castello*'s many antique clocks and was an expert in the mechanism that lowered the priceless chandeliers, was at the other end of the room, intent on a control panel hidden in the wall.

And Charlotte, looking far too seductive in a grey skirt that sculpted her buttocks as she leaned forward, was up a ladder, reaching for a cluster of crystal drops.

His pulse quickened and his mouth dried.

What was it with this woman and ladders? Hadn't she had enough of heights in the library?

He opened his mouth to order her down, then stopped. No need to startle her. Instead he stalked across the room, vaguely aware of heads turning, but he didn't stop till he reached the base of the ladder. Even then she didn't notice him. Slowly she descended, one hand on the ladder as she cradled precious crystal to her chest. It wasn't until she reached him, his hand braced on the ladder where she was about to put hers, that she stopped.

'Alessio!'

She sounded breathless, and as her gaze caught his he read more than surprise. It was the same expression he'd seen the day he'd held her in his arms. Yearning. Excitement. Arousal.

His heart leapt.

That was why his feelings for her ate him up. Because he knew he wasn't the only one attracted.

He'd told himself that day in the library that he'd imagined it and she'd only wanted comfort. But he was a man who knew women and desire. Charlotte desired him, though she tried to hide it behind a facade of professionalism.

And he, a man used to indulging his desires, found it pure torture, holding back.

Because she was his employee.

Because he had a duty of care.

Because he was ultimately responsible for his wife's death, and he had no right to enjoy the delights of a sexual liaison when Antonia lay dead in the cold earth.

He drew a slow, shuddering breath and stepped back.

He was tainted, and he couldn't spread that miasma to an innocent woman.

'Are you all right?' she murmured.

That was another thing he hated. Her perceptiveness. Charlotte saw things in him no one else did. Emotions. Weaknesses.

Alessio couldn't get his head around it. He was used to being controlled, contained and unreadable.

Even Anna, who'd known him from birth, knew better than to prod about his well-being. But this woman who gave the impression of being the perfect employee, competent, efficient and adept at anticipating his needs, crossed vital personal boundaries.

He abhorred that. It made him feel... vulnerable.'With me. Now.'

He spun on his heel and marched from the room. He didn't pause until he was on the flagstone terrace on the west side of the building, where water lapped below the balustrade.

Even here Charlotte Symonds had made her mark. Last time he'd been here, the great stone urns had been empty. Now they were planted with bright red flowers, so vivid in the sunlight they made him think of days long ago when parties had spilled out here, the air filled with laughter and music.

The memory hurt.

Damn it, everything hurt. Surely life had been easier when there'd been nothing to interrupt his solitude, or make him yearn for things he couldn't have.

Alessio stalked to the edge, sparing a glance for the deep, still water that hemmed in his world.

Finally he turned, leaning against the balustrade to survey the woman who'd followed him, mastering the urge to take her in his arms and kiss her. It was too tempting. He could *feel* her body against his, the waft of her breath on his face, the softness of her mouth as she pressed close and begged for more.

His head cleared, and he saw her face was unreadable. It struck him that Charlotte, like he, had practice at hiding thoughts. Because of her work? Or because of something else? What secrets did she conceal?

'What's going on?' he asked.

'Going on?' Behind that bland expression, he read something in her eyes. Turmoil. Guilt?

'Yes, going on.' Alessio gestured to the pieces of crystal she clutched to her breast. 'That's not the usual dusting you're doing. I didn't give you permission to open up the ballroom.'

Charlotte stiffened, and despite his annoyance, he admired the way her chin came up and she looked down that unremarkable nose at him, undaunted. Inevitably, his admiration took the form of a burst of heat low in his body. He shifted his weight, planting his feet wider.

'I wasn't aware I needed your permission to enter the room. You and Anna said I had free access to the whole building, apart from your study when you're working.'

'You're avoiding the issue, Charlotte.' He took his time, savouring the taste of her name, hearing his voice drop to a hungry drawl. He was rewarded with a rosy blush to her cheeks as her gaze fell to his mouth. His groin tightened.

The man he'd once been would have scorned such a cheap triumph as making her blush with awareness, but the man he'd become revelled in knowing she responded to him. That this sexual awareness wasn't one-sided.

'The question isn't permission to go into the ballroom. It's what you're doing there.' He folded his arms and narrowed his eyes. 'You're up to something.'

She bit her lip, and he stifled a groan at the way that drew attention to her lush pink mouth.

'There seemed no harm in a proper spring clean. We're being extraordinarily careful. Every piece of glass is numbered and—'

'That's not in question.' He kept his voice even. 'What. Are. You. Up. To?'

Charlotte sighed and walked to a nearby table, carefully depositing the antique crystals. The sunlight caught them, casting a rainbow reflection across her face. But when she turned, there was no hint of radiance on her features, just wariness.

'I found a list Anna had left in a drawer in the kitchen. A list of…plans.'

'Go on.'

'The main item was preparation for the island's spring festival.'

A weight plunged through Alessio's gut. 'There's

been no festival for years.' Not since he and Antonia moved here from Rome.

'So I gather.' At his stare, she spread her hands wide. 'I asked Mario about it. He said it was enormous fun, the highlight of the whole year, not just for the islanders but for those beyond the lake.'

'*Was* being the operative word.' This was no time for inane festivities.

'So Anna hadn't talked with you about it?'

'Not this year.' Alessio gritted his teeth. She'd raised the possibility last year, but he'd squashed it. He hadn't been able to bear the idea of noise and gaiety, his island invaded by partygoers. Not when he needed peace and solitude.

'I see.' Again that almost martial look from under her finely arched brows. 'You refused last year, and she didn't have time to raise it again before she went to Rome.'

Or she'd been biding her time, waiting for the best opportunity to raise it, hoping to catch him in a weak moment.

'You guessed she hadn't,' he said slowly, watching her expression shutter. 'That's why you didn't mention it. What was the plan? To get so far along with the preparations, you hoped I wouldn't have the heart to put a stop to it?'

Her flush deepened, but instead of apologising, she folded her arms, mirroring his stance and inadvertently giving him a tantalising glimpse of cleavage where a button had come undone as she'd unburdened herself of the crystal.

'Why would you stop it, Alessio? Is it such a bad thing?' Despite her challenging stance, far from being confrontational, Charlotte's tone turned soft. As if she pondered and was concerned about his motivations. As if she guessed at some of the black burden of remorse weighing on his soul.

He pulled in his wandering thoughts. No one understood.

'This isn't up for debate. It's my decision, and my answer is no.'

For a full minute, silence expanded between them. In the distance, he heard a motorboat crossing the lake, and nearer, a bird calling to its mate.

'You know how much this celebration means to people here?'

Alessio stood taller. How dared she assume to lecture him on *his* people?

But she'd known about the need for a new commercial opportunity for local artisans. She'd known about Mario's great-nephew. Things Alessio should have known. Anger rose at himself more than anyone else.

'The festival was always at the prerogative of the Conte since he pays for it.'

Her eyes widened. 'You're worried about the cost?'

'Of course not!' He couldn't believe she'd thought that or had the temerity to ask. Money had never been a problem for his family, and under his stewardship, the family business had gone from strength to strength.

She shook her head, her eyes never leaving his. 'So it's just that you, personally, don't want to be bothered? I can do a lot of the work, and I know from speaking to some of the locals that we could set up a committee—'

'You've already discussed this with them?' Alessio's voice was sharp with warning.

Charlotte heard it. Her crossed arms and tight shoulders now looked defensive rather than challenging.

'After I asked Mario about it, he mentioned it to some of the others. A couple of them spoke to me.'

In other words, she'd gone behind his back. Alessio's chest rose and fell as he reined in anger.

Anna had asked about a festival last year, but she'd understood, as had the other islanders, that such a celebration was inappropriate given his loss.

'This is none of your business. You're an outsider.'

Once again Charlotte's cheeks flushed pink. Then the colour faded, leaving her features pale and taut. Piling another layer of guilt onto Alessio's conscience.

'I apologise if I've overstepped the mark.' Her voice was brittle but not, he realised, with apology. 'I've followed the guidelines you and Anna set. Given your instructions not to interrupt you,

I haven't had a chance to raise the issue with you before now.' She paused as if daring him to disagree. Her eyes flashed fire, and his skin prickled. 'So I decided to start at least preparing the *castello* in case you agreed.'

Her breasts rose against her pale shirt, and Alessio couldn't help but wonder what it would be like if Charlotte shared some of the passion she tried to suppress with a man. With him. His groin grew tight and heavy, and that annoyed him even more.

Alessio was trapped in a never-ending cycle. Solitude brought little relief. But being with people again brought more problems. He couldn't even manage his feelings for his housekeeper. He was wracked by libidinous urges he couldn't relieve and bound by past mistakes to live out his penance alone.

'Well, you know now. No festival.'

'Even though the people here want it? Just because you want to bury yourself here, don't they deserve their celebration?'

Alessio stared. Was she accusing him of being selfish? She hadn't used the word, but the implication was clear. He saw the judgement in those blazing eyes. As for *burying himself*, no one bar his Great-Aunt Beatrice had the nerve to say such a thing.

'Wouldn't the festival be another, bigger chance to showcase the island and local businesses? A showcase they badly need. I've heard people come from Rome and beyond for the celebrations. It would be a huge boost locally. From what I've heard, they badly need that.'

The truth of her words stopped his automatic refusal.

Alessio grew hot and then cold with shame. He'd made a point recently of visiting his neighbours, gauging how they were doing. Most were highly skilled craftspeople, many in specialised fields. A few had weathered the recent economic difficulties well, but others hadn't. He had plans to help them but hadn't even considered the festival as a springboard for those plans. Now he realised it was an obvious starting point.

Not that anyone had mentioned the festival to him. Because they respected his mourning? Or because they knew he'd dismiss it out of hand?

Self-absorbed. Selfish. The words circled in his head.

Had his rejection of the outside world meant he held his own people to ransom? His gut curdled, and his mouth tugged down in a grimace self-disgust.

He spun around and planted his hands on the stone balustrade, feeling his lowering head drag heavily at his shoulders. Feeling the lead in his belly as he stared at the beautiful, unforgiving waters that had shaped his life.

'If you're concerned about being with strangers…' She faltered to a stop as he swung around.

He'd had enough of Charlotte analysing him. It was clear she believed he was hiding away, a skulking hermit too scared to leave his home or meet others.

Yet you haven't left the island in three years.

That didn't matter. That was his choice. He had everything he needed here. Yet her pity grated.

Out of the plethora of emotions bombarding him, guilt, dismay, determination and even unwilling arousal as he watched Charlotte's breasts rise with each quick breath, the strongest was anger. At himself above all, for being blind and thoughtless, burying himself in his own needs instead of doing his duty by his people.

Anger at Charlotte too, for seeing what he hadn't and making him face it. He knew he was at risk of shooting the messenger. She hadn't actually done anything wrong, but his fury needed an outlet.

Alessio leaned back against the balustrade, planting his hands on the stonework and crossing his ankles with a nonchalance he didn't feel. She thought him pitiable? A shadow of the man he'd been, scared to face the world again?

Battered pride rose. It was easier to cling to that than admit she was right and thank her for forcing him to see what he'd done.

'Very well. The festival will go ahead.' Her eyes rounded and her lips, those sweet lips that haunted his dreams, curved in the beginnings of a smile. 'I'll take care of it.' He'd get started today. 'Except for the grand spring ball. That's what you're cleaning the chandeliers for, isn't it?'

Before Charlotte could respond, he continued. 'There'll be several hundred guests. Some locals but many more from elsewhere. The cream of European high society.'

His mouth twisted. He had no doubt every invitation would be accepted. Everyone would be eager to see how he fared after his wife's death. To try to discover the truth of the rumours they'd all been spreading.

'Apart from the invitation list, I'll leave every detail of that in your capable hands. As well as spring cleaning the *castello*, of course.' Alessio smirked, knowing preparation for the gala ball alone usually took a team months of work. Charlotte's arrested expression told him she was beginning to guess as much.

Good. That would keep her busy and out of his way.

'If you manage that to my satisfaction, I'll give you a glowing reference to take to your next position.'

He straightened and headed for the *castello* entrance.

'One more thing.' He paused beside her, knowing he was being unreasonable, knowing he'd owe her a massive apology later, yet unable to prevent himself taking out his simmering fury on the woman who'd brought all this to a head. 'I want you there through it all, but not behind the scenes. I want you front and centre as my hostess.'

It was one thing to work for rich hotel clients, quite another to mix with them as an equal in a social setting. Charlotte Symonds would learn how tough that was.

Maybe then she'd have some tiny inkling of how appalling it was for him to face the prospect of society's curious gaze. The whispers and gossip. The false sympathy hiding eagerness for juicy details of his personal life.

If he had to suffer through the spring festivities, so could she. With luck she'd resign when she realised what she was facing. Then maybe he'd have some measure of peace in his home.

The thought should have pleased him. Yet as he stalked inside, Alessio's mood was grimmer than ever.

CHAPTER EIGHT

CHARLOTTE LIFTED HER head and stretched cramped fingers. She'd missed the sunset again, her favourite time of day. Now the island and lake were bathed in deepening indigo.

The place had a special quality she'd felt from the beginning. A beauty and peacefulness that she appreciated more the longer she stayed.

Even now, with preparations for the festival in full swing. The silence was regularly broken by the sound of power tools, boats and voices as structures were made for outdoor celebrations and seating to view the boat races. For the peace was about far more than silence. The island drew her, welcomed her. She'd miss it when she left in two months.

Her mouth flattened and she rose, rolling stiff shoulders and walking to her window at the sound of voices.

Alessio approached down the cobbled lane with three other men. They stood close, gesticulating as they talked, pointing to the shoreline and arguing the merits of putting banked seating there. Alessio murmured something, and there was a roar of laughter.

This wasn't the first time she'd witnessed his easy interaction with the locals, though a mere week ago they'd seemed more reserved, as if they weren't used to his company.

Had he cut himself off from *everyone*? Her heart squeezed.

Clearly, though, they respected and liked him, and he felt the same about them. No wonder they'd protected his privacy. Alessio might enjoy adopting the role of lofty lord of the manor with her sometimes, but he wasn't always so stiff-necked.

Something pulled in Charlotte's chest. Pleasure, seeing him interacting easily when once he'd been so reclusive? Delight at his resonant, deep chuckle that, even from this distance, melted some of the tension in her weary body?

She tried to summon anger. It was his fault she was exhausted, working through the evenings. He'd set her an almost impossible challenge because she'd dared to interfere.

Still, Alessio undid her as no man ever had.

Just as well they didn't spend enough time together for him to notice. Though, to his credit, he increasingly sought her out to check how she was faring and, she suspected, to give her the chance to ask for help. But she'd been too proud, determined to prove herself.

Her father had consistently underrated her, jeering at what he called the humdrum domestic skills she'd learned from her mother. Charlotte didn't know if she was working herself to the bone to prove herself to Alessio or to the father who'd never see the fruits of her labour.

And she thought Alessio had problems, letting the past shadow the present too much!

Face it. It's not your father you're trying to impress. It's Alessio. You want him to be stunned by how wonderful the ball is, how successful and grand. You want him to look at you with admiration and respect.

She watched the men walk away and drew a deep breath, scented with sweet-smelling flowers.

Slowly Charlotte turned, her gaze falling on rich, blue velvet. The dress she was making for the ball.

Alessio had wanted to punish her for daring to question him. She'd read his temper. No doubt he'd expected her to be out of her depth and turn to him, begging for help.

Her lips twisted. For once her past was her secret weapon instead of a burden. She'd been born and bred for events like this. Even in her teens, she'd worn designer evening gowns.

Later, after she'd spurned her father's schemes and had no money, she'd learned to sew her own clothes. She could have dipped into her savings now to buy something special but had no time to travel to a city boutique. Nor did she trust online shopping. This had to be something stunning, made specifically for her.

Because you want Alessio to look at you with more than admiration and respect. You want him to want you. You want him to feel that same trembling tug of awareness.

Charlotte pressed a hand to her thundering heart.

It was ridiculous. She'd seen photos of his glamorous wife with a film star's poise and beauty to match. Her glossy dark hair, sculpted features and stunning body cast other women into the shade.

No ordinary woman could compare.

Yet there'd been times when Charlotte felt Alessio's hungry stare. Been *sure* he experienced that desperate attraction too. But he'd pulled back, and she didn't know what to do with the jumble of emotions and longing inside her. It felt like her skin was too tight, and nothing would soothe her but his touch.

She should be grateful he'd withdrawn. An affair with her boss was impossible. It broke every professional rule.

Yet an unfamiliar part of her, oblivious to propriety or duty or even the future, craved the impossible.

For the first time, she desired a man with all her being. He infuriated her yet drew her like metal to a magnet.

She wanted Alessio to find her desirable in her own right. Not as simply convenient as she'd been to the man who'd considered marrying her to cement a deal with her father. Or to the hotel guests who'd assumed too much about the services hotel staff provided.

Even if it could go nowhere. Even if Alessio still grieved for the wife he'd lost.

Shame burned in her, yet that didn't stop this yearning. It was utterly selfish, but to know just once that he too felt this, even though he'd never pursue it, was vital.

To her self-esteem? Surely not. She didn't need a man to make her feel good about herself.

But maybe it was time to come out of the self-imposed hibernation she'd embraced after her mother died. She'd been grieving and lost when her father tried to force her into an engagement. Her first and only sexual experience had been the deliberate, crude groping of a man who thought himself entitled to her body because her father badly wanted to do business with him.

Charlotte smoothed her palm across the rich fabric. She imagined it against her skin, but from there her imagination leapt to the idea of Alessio's strong, capable hands stroking her flesh.

Fabric crumpled under clutching fingers as she shivered. Primal instinct warned that she courted disaster. Instead of trying to attract Alessio, she should find an excuse to leave. No matter how much explaining she had to do in her next job.

That would be sensible. Trouble was, for the first time in forever, Charlotte didn't feel sensible.

'There you are. I've been searching for you.'

Charlotte sat back on her haunches and looked

up. Her head swam, and she told herself it was because she'd been leaning deep into the cupboard in the butler's pantry. Not because Alessio filled the doorway, making her pulse gallop.

'I'm taking inventory of the silverware for supper on the night of the ball.' She held up a huge platter engraved with his coat of arms. There were at least a dozen such platters, plus tureens, gravy boats, goblets, cutlery and a multitude of other items.

'If you need more, let me know and I'll open one of the vaults.'

One of the vaults?

'I'm sure that won't be necessary.' Charlotte scrambled up, feeling at a disadvantage on the floor. 'What can I help you with?'

She kept her gaze on his chin rather than his eyes, but that was a mistake because she found herself staring at those superbly sculpted lips and remembering the feel of his hair-roughened jaw beneath her fingertips.

'For once, Charlotte, it's me wanting to help you.'

Startled, she looked straight into fathomless eyes and felt the tide of longing ripple through her bloodstream.

Yes, please. Can you soothe away this jittery feeling? Maybe with a kiss?

As if that would ever happen. Even if Alessio was attracted, he was obviously grieving for his wife. And he never forgot they were employer and employee.

Yet the way he looked at her with all that lambent heat…

It took a moment to realise he was holding out a card. Gingerly she took it. Embossed in gold were the name and contact details of a world-renowned couturier in Milan.

'A driver will take you tomorrow to be fitted for a ball gown.' He paused. 'It was remiss of me not to organise it sooner.'

'Thank you, but I don't need it. I have a dress sorted.' Though it wouldn't be a patch on a designer gown.

Alessio shook his head. 'I invited…ordered you to attend.' His mouth firmed. 'I apologise. I wasn't at my best that day, and I took it out on you. But I'm not so unreasonable as to expect you to pay for a formal dress that you'll only wear once, because I demanded your presence.'

Charlotte stared, torn between competing impulses. To smile and accept this olive branch. Because it was just that, with an admission of guilt, no less. Yet at the same time, it rankled that he assumed she'd never wear a ball dress after she left here. Because her life was about serving others, not ever being the belle of the ball.

'Thank you. Apology accepted. But there really is no need. I have a dress that's suitable.'

She'd tried the jewel-coloured gown on last night

and been stunned. For the first time in her adult life, Charlotte had felt glamorous and seductive. Not at all like the practical, down-to-earth woman she really was.

Alessio frowned as if he didn't believe her, or maybe didn't trust her to know what would pass muster at such an exclusive event.

'Don't worry, Alessio. I've served at some very elite events. I won't embarrass you.'

'I know you won't.' The certainty in his voice surprised her. 'What colour is the dress?'

'Deep blue.'

He angled his head as if to get a better look at her. Why? She hadn't altered. She wore her usual uniform with her hair neatly up, the barest hint of make-up and no jewellery. Yet as his scrutiny touched her face and hair, dipping briefly to skim her body, that too-familiar heat built in her pelvis.

'If you change your mind about the dress, let me know.' Charlotte nodded. 'And as of today, I've assigned someone to assist you.' He raised his palm as if anticipating a protest. 'No arguments. You're doing a fine job, but I don't want you too exhausted to attend the ball.'

Then, without waiting for further argument, he turned on his heel and disappeared, leaving Charlotte confused. Was he just ensuring he had a hostess available on the night? Or was he genuinely concerned for her?

He *had* apologised for being unreasonable and

making her solely responsible for the ball. And he could have offered to get her a dress from a nearby boutique without arranging for her to go to a world-class designer.

She hugged the massive silver tray to herself. The trouble was, she wanted him to be aware of her as a woman when every sensible bone in her body knew that was dangerous. What she felt for him was dangerous.

She'd see the ball done and then leave. Because staying, feeling the way she did about her employer, was a recipe for disaster.

Charlotte paused outside Alessio's study, smoothing her long skirt. When she'd looked in the mirror, she'd seen a woman she didn't know. Someone glamorous and intriguing. Not at all like a housekeeper, but like...

Who? Cinderella?

She snorted. She might be going to the ball, but she was still staff. Nothing changed that. Her dress wouldn't compare with the haute couture of the guests. And when every other invitee was tucked up in bed after the festivities, she'd be the one organising the clean-up.

Tonight is work.

But as she rapped on Alessio's door she couldn't scotch a tingle of anticipation at the thought of standing beside him to receive his guests.

'Come in, Charlotte.' His low voice curled

around her, and strangely, her flutter of nerves settled.

He had his back to her. But he swung around as she approached, and she faltered to a halt midway across the room.

He was magnificent.

Her gaze roved his features, taking in neatly trimmed hair and scrupulously shaved skin that revealed a proud, well-shaped chin. His formal evening suit, snowy shirt and silk bow tie set off his austere good looks so well that he literally stole her breath.

Charlotte pressed a hand to her churning abdomen, trying to still her reaction.

She'd dreamed of Alessio as a marauding pirate who swept her off her feet and did things to her no man ever had. She'd thought nothing could surpass that secret fantasy. Now she realised her error. In formal clothes, the Conte Dal Lago was the sexiest, most handsome man she'd ever met.

And then he smiled.

Pleasure curled his mouth and lit his eyes, and her breath snagged in cramped lungs.

'You look beautiful,' he told her.

It was ridiculous to be undone by his words. But no one had called her beautiful and really meant it since her mother died. Passing compliments from men looking for quick sex didn't count. Charlotte viewed her round face and ordinary features as pleasant, not outstanding, though her blond hair was a pretty colour.

But meeting Alessio's gleaming eyes, she believed he meant it. She stood taller.

'Thank you. So do you.'

He laughed, the sound snagging in her chest. He didn't seem like the proud, reclusive aristocrat now. 'You're very kind.'

Not kind at all. It was an understatement. She hurried on, needing to change the subject. 'You wanted to see me?'

'I did. I wanted to loan you this to wear.'

Charlotte looked down to the case in his hands. Inside lay a necklace of flawless sapphires, the centre one as large as a pigeon's egg.

She couldn't prevent an audible gasp. 'You were going to lend that to *me*?'

He put the case on the desk beside him, where the gemstones glowed under the overhead light. 'You're my hostess tonight, and I—'

'Was afraid I wouldn't measure up?'

Alessio's eyes narrowed. 'No. I was going to say I regretted putting you in a situation where you might feel out of your depth.' He paused as if choosing his words. 'I wanted to make amends and do what I could to make the evening feel less daunting.'

Charlotte was stunned. She'd seen a change in him as he spent more time with others, busy working with his community. But this was an extraordinarily generous offer. She had no doubt the gems were priceless heirlooms.

'You said you were wearing blue.' His voice dipped and dragged through her middle. 'I wanted to see you wearing this. Sapphires would be perfect against your creamy skin.'

She swallowed hard. The way he spoke, it sounded like he'd made a study of her complexion. Deep inside, a tight knot of pent-up emotion loosened and frayed.

'But I see my offer is unnecessary. Your own jewellery is perfect.'

Her hand went to her pendant. 'Thank you. It's precious to me.'

It was the only jewellery she had from her mother. Her father kept the rest locked away, though it was technically Charlotte's. Because Charlotte had dared to defy his wishes in not marrying the man of his choice. Her father couldn't abide being crossed.

Alessio moved closer. 'May I?' He nodded to the necklace.

'I...of course.'

Deft fingers lifted the pendant from her décolletage, but that barely-there brush of skin on skin felt like so much more. Charlotte clamped her lips together and fought a shiver of reaction.

'Baroque pearls and a fine ruby. Exquisite.'

He stood so close his words were a puff of warm air across her skin, and she caught the slight tang of clean male skin, cedar and exotic incense. Valiantly she fought not to meet his gaze, but the draw of him was too strong.

Had Alessio's eyes always been that dark? Not with anger or impatience but something she'd never seen before.

She was leaning closer when she realised what she was doing and stepped back. Instantly he released her pendant and it fell to her breast, warm from his hand.

Her breathing faltered. To her overwrought senses, it felt like he'd touched her.

'It's an unusual design. Several hundred years old.'

Of course he could date it. He specialised in antique treasures. 'I was told it came from a much larger piece that was broken up.'

Wealthy as her mother's family had been, they'd fallen on difficult financial times. Until Charlotte's mother married a successful businessman. But, as Charlotte and her mother had learned to their cost, money didn't guarantee happiness.

Since her mother's death, Charlotte had kept the piece in a bank deposit box, afraid of losing it or being tempted to sell it when she'd struggled to make ends meet. She'd only retrieved it before coming to Italy, not wanting to leave it behind.

'Well, you wear it admirably.' Alessio inclined his head. 'Now, shall we go?'

Charlotte was just full of surprises, Alessio mused, torn between rampant curiosity, admiration and lust. And a piercing sliver of annoyance at having been naive enough to underestimate her. He didn't enjoy feeling like a fool.

Far from being out of her depth, she'd come alive at the ball, as if born to such grand events. He'd had no reason to feel guilty, berating himself for placing her in an impossible situation.

Somehow she combined overseeing the staff and catering and acting the gracious hostess as if it were easy.

Alessio could attest that dealing with his guests' curiosity was anything but easy. His champagne turned sour and his flesh prickled whenever he faced the never-ending curiosity about his dead wife and his own solitude. Or felt clutching female hands on his arm as one eager socialite after another made it clear they would happily distract him from his sorrows.

He shuddered, repulsed, and his gaze turned again to the enigma who was his housekeeper, waltzing down the centre of the room in the arms of one of Italy's most eligible bachelors.

Alessio's hand tightened around his wineglass, and he shoved his other bunching fist into his pocket.

Charlotte looked serene and carefree. And it didn't feel like an act. It felt real.

As real as the way she'd chatted easily with billionaire businesspeople, minor royalty and trophy wives. She'd made introductions, guided an eligible dance partner towards a reserved young woman, and fielded queries about her employment here with good humour and poise.

More than once, she'd even deflected the conversation of someone intent on interrogating him about Antonia.

As if he needed protection!

He was the Conte Dal Lago. He fought his own battles.

Yet it was curiously…nice having Charlotte wield that gracious smile like a weapon on his behalf.

Who is this woman?

She couldn't have learned those skills in housekeeping school. For all the time he'd spent fixated on her, he'd done nothing to uncover her past. It was clear she had almost as many secrets as he.

'If the wind changes, your face will stay like that.' Great-Aunt Beatrice's hoarse chuckle made him turn. 'Not that you look ugly. In fact, that Scandinavian princess seems quite taken with your scowl.'

'Beatrice.' He smoothed out his expression. 'I hope you're enjoying yourself.'

'I've never had so much fun.' The gleam in her black eyes would make a lesser man uneasy. 'I find her delightful, by the way, your Charlotte.'

Alessio was about to snap that she wasn't his Charlotte but knew any sign of emotion would be minutely scrutinised. He didn't need Beatrice, who already interfered too much, to realise he lusted after his housekeeper. Or that he was jealous of the never-ending line of men eager to dance with her.

He'd let it be known he wouldn't dance tonight. It was tough enough, facing the glare of avid public interest. Keeping some personal distance was vital.

Beatrice didn't wait for a reply. 'She and I had a lovely chat earlier. So…informative.' He tensed, until she added with a sideways look, 'About embroidery, mainly. I *knew* that gift must have been someone else's idea. You wouldn't know embroidery silk from tapestry wool.'

'I'm pleased you like it.'

The old girl raised her eyebrows at his laconic answer. But he refused to discuss Charlotte. With anyone.

'I like the way she's shaken things up around here.'

Shaken things up? Shaken *him* up, more like.

'Such an interesting background she must have too. I was chatting earlier with George Somersby. He was surprised to learn Charlotte's your housekeeper. He remembers her attending exclusive black-tie events at a stately home in England. But she definitely wasn't a member of staff.'

Alessio's eyes widened. It was more than *interesting*. It was more proof that she was an enigma. He shot an assessing look at Charlotte, circling elegantly in her partner's arms, and felt his jaw clench.

His great-aunt nodded briskly as if confirming something. 'Good night, Alessio. Giorgia's ready to leave.' He'd invited Beatrice to stay overnight, the only person to receive such an invitation, but she preferred to stay with an old friend. 'It's been… illuminating.' Her grin was sly, and Alessio was instantly on guard. 'I can't remember a more entertaining evening.'

After escorting Beatrice out, he returned to the doorway, surveying the scene.

The ballroom glittered, every glass and mirror polished. Flowers in decorative jardinières and enormous formal arrangements scented the air. In the supper room, visible through open doors, tables covered in finest linen and antique silver groaned under a spread of gourmet delicacies.

Chatter filled the air, and everywhere he saw smiles. The ball, the opening event of the festival, proved he'd done right, agreeing to it.

Charlotte had been right.

Musicians performed in the minstrels' gallery, and the floor was packed with people in their finery, from locals in neat suits and pretty dresses to the monied elite in bespoke tailoring, fabulous jewels and designer gowns.

Amongst them all, Charlotte stood out.

It wasn't merely the way the light caught the rich gold of her hair. Or the way said hair was styled in a luxurious, softened upsweep that revealed her slender neck yet left tendrils free. It gave her a seductive look, inevitably making him imagine her just risen from bed.

Her dress was the rich blue of lapis lazuli, shaping her body like a lover's hands before falling in folds to the floor. A band of fabric rose in a V from deep over her cleavage to the points of each shoulder, making him wonder how securely that bodice was held up. It left a wide swathe of perfect pale skin bare.

Except it wasn't pale now. She glowed with exertion from dancing. Or maybe from delight at the sweet nothings that Roman playboy was whispering in her ear.

Pain exploded in Alessio's jaw from grinding molars. He wanted to stalk across and wrest her away from those grasping hands. Pull her into his arms and then...

It's not dancing you have in mind, is it?

All night, every time he'd seen her in the arms of another man, his tension had screwed tighter. He remembered holding Charlotte against him. How right it had felt. How much more he'd wanted. And how wrong that was.

Alessio stood, fighting the impulse to make a scene and march off with Charlotte in his arms while the world gawked. Then he turned and pushed his way from the room.

Charlotte caught Alessio's eyes on her. Again. All evening she'd felt that spark of heat and turned to find him glaring at her. So much for the sensual awareness she'd hoped for. With the guests, he was all smiles and urbane charm. It was only when he looked at her that he frowned.

What had she done wrong? The evening had turned out wonderfully. Even his dragon of an aunt had proved herself impressed and approving, albeit disconcertingly outspoken.

She couldn't think why he wasn't thrilled. She'd worked so hard and deserved his appreciation. More than one guest had said it was the best party they'd attended in years.

But it's his feedback that matters, isn't it?

Alessio scowled and turned away. Charlotte's heart plummeted even as she shored up her indignation. But she was too deflated to concentrate on anger at the man she'd tried to impress, not as his efficient employee but as a seductive, alluring woman.

She focused on her companion, discreetly moving his roving hand higher. Not long to go now. Soon she could ditch the long dress and heels and put on work clothes for the clean-up.

So much for romantic yearnings.

So much for Cinderella.

They stood together at the main entrance to the *castello*, waving goodbye to the last of the guests heading to the boats that would take them to their luxury accommodations. While the Conte Dal Lago had opened his doors for a fabulous celebration that guests would talk about for years to come, there'd be no overnight guests.

The chatter and laughter died away, and still Alessio said nothing. Not one word of praise. In silence he closed and bolted the vast iron-studded doors.

Charlotte had had enough. She'd done her best, but clearly it wasn't enough to satisfy him. And it wasn't as if the night were over. She had hours of work ahead.

She spun on her heel, lifting the long skirts that had made her feel, for a little while, like a princess in a fairy tale. Her jaw clenched at her futile imaginings. Nothing would make her more than his domestic drudge. She flattened her mouth, fanning anger at her own stupidity.

'Where are you going?' Alessio's voice was sharp.

She didn't bother to turn back, instead marching towards the grand staircase. 'To my room to get changed, ready to supervise the clean-up.'

'No.'

Nothing else. Just a single word.

'Pardon?' She was forced to swing around, and discovered him right there, so close she could see the hint of tiny dark bristles beginning to form on his jaw.

'I cancelled tonight's clean-up and sent everyone home.'

'You did what?'

'It can wait till tomorrow.'

'Everyone will be busy tomorrow. There are boat races and a festival and—'

'Then the cleaning can wait till after the festival.'

Charlotte opened her mouth to argue. Then she read his expression, and her breath disappeared. A finger of disquiet tracked down her spine, making her shiver.

He looked…dangerous.

Yet she felt no impulse to flee. On the contrary…

'Aren't you going to ask me why I sent them away, Charlotte?' Alessio's voice was silky smooth, yet tight with whatever emotion clamped his jaw.

The air between them thickened, and she had to moisten her suddenly dry mouth. 'Why, Alessio?'

His eyes flared as her voice turned husky on his name. Then his mouth curled in a harsh smile, and he stepped close, his arm encircling her waist and drawing her up against him. 'Because of *this*.'

CHAPTER NINE

ALESSIO'S ARM AROUND her felt shockingly familiar, stopping her angry retort.

Charlotte might be infuriated and confused, but she knew what she wanted.

This. The weight of his arm around her waist, pulling her hard against his lean, muscular frame. The press of powerful thighs against hers. The spark of awareness that turned his usually cool green gaze to fire.

She felt that fire inside, racing along her veins, pooling in her pelvis, heating breasts that seemed to swell and press against the tight fabric of her bodice.

'What *do* you want, Alessio? You need to be more specific.'

She was amazed to hear herself sound so calm.

His eyes crinkled at the corners. 'With pleasure.' Did she imagine he gave the word *pleasure* lingering emphasis? 'It's a ball, Charlotte. I want to dance with you.'

She shook her head, spirits plummeting. Was he making fun of her? 'The ball's over. We could have danced earlier.'

She ordered her unresponsive feet to step back, but they didn't move.

'Impossible. If I'd danced with you, then I'd have

been obliged to dance with others.' His eyes held hers, and his voice deepened to a luscious rumble. 'I didn't want to dance with anyone else. Just you.'

As if she alone, among all those sophisticated women, attracted him. Charlotte swallowed and discovered her throat had constricted. Her heart beat too fast, and her thoughts scrambled.

Danger, screamed a warning voice in her head. *But, oh, what glorious danger.*

When he looked at her that way, Alessio undermined all her caution. After years protecting herself, maybe it was time to live a little. To choose danger instead of safety.

Still she resisted. 'There's no music.'

Alessio took her resisting hand and placed it on his shoulder, where her fingers instantly spread and clung, absorbing his heat and hard strength. He took her other hand, lifting it in a waltz hold.

'You can't hear the music?' He drew her closer. 'Listen to your heartbeat.'

Then they were moving, slowly but in perfect unison in a circle that took them from the vaulted entry hall into the brilliantly lit ballroom.

Charlotte was floating, the steps coming easily, without thought. As if they'd danced together a thousand times, their bodies totally attuned.

Alessio swung her faster, and now they swirled down the grand room, her skirts flaring, their legs pressing close, and not once did he lift his gaze from hers. She could almost hear the music, its powerful rhythm urging her on. They reached the end of the room, and his arm tightened around her waist, swinging her up for a second off the floor.

A laugh escaped her. The sound of pure joy as they circled back along the polished floor, faster and faster. Yet Charlotte felt totally secure in Alessio's embrace, ready to go where he led, caught up in heady excitement.

'Why were you angry?' she asked him. 'You marched out of here in a temper.'

The words emerged as a gasp, but Alessio didn't slow. If anything he hugged her closer, spinning them faster on the next turn. Charlotte didn't care. Never had a dance felt like this, like they were flying.

For a moment, for two, it seemed he wouldn't answer. Then they slowed to a more decorous pace. 'The simple answer?'

His eyes glinted, and arousal arrowed to her core. Charlotte nodded. It was more and more difficult to concentrate on words. 'Simple will do.'

'Frustration.' His chest rose high in the first indication that their reckless speed affected him. But his next words proved it wasn't that shortening his breath. 'I wanted you in *my* arms, Charlotte. Not dancing with every womaniser and layabout in Italy.'

Charlotte stumbled, and Alessio's hold tightened. Their steps slowed until they barely moved.

'They weren't all womanisers and layabouts.'

He huffed out a laugh, and the sound stroked deep inside her. 'I wanted to throw them out when I saw how they looked at you.'

Her eyes grew huge. Alessio had been *jealous*? Her chest clogged. 'And are you enjoying it now, dancing with me?'

To her surprise, he shook his head. Charlotte pulled back in his embrace, but still Alessio held her securely.

'I was. But it's not enough.' He swallowed hard, and to her astonishment, this man who'd always controlled every situation looked suddenly desperate. 'I want more, Charlotte, much more. Too much.'

That teasing smile was gone, his features harsh as he frowned down at her. Then she turned cold as he released her, sliding his arm away and stepping back so her hand on his shoulder dropped to her side.

His voice was rough when he spoke again. 'This was a mistake. You work for me. I remind myself all the time, but tonight I keep forgetting and—'

'Couldn't we pretend for tonight that I don't?' Did he hear her longing? 'Couldn't we pretend I'm someone else?'

He shook his head so vehemently that obstinate lock of hair tumbled forward over his brow. All night Alessio had looked perfectly groomed, perfectly in command. Now he was more like the marauder she'd first met.

'No pretending. It's you I want, Charlotte. The woman who drives me to distraction with her un-flappable efficiency. Who makes even navy trousers and flat shoes sexy! A woman of secrets who's anything but a simple housekeeper.' He watched her jump of surprise. 'Oh, yes, I see more than you think.'

His words were a potent caress, smoothing doubts and fears, stroking her sensitised skin and stoking the need deep inside.

How could she resist a man who said such things and meant them? It was rare for Alessio to let down his guard, but now he did, enough for her to see the truth in his eyes. The raw hunger, the loneliness that matched hers.

Charlotte's heart squeezed. 'If you see so much, then you know how I feel.'

He wasn't letting her off the hook. 'Tell me.'

She held his gaze. 'I want you, Alessio. I've tried to pretend there's nothing between us, but it doesn't work. I've never had a sexual relationship with an employer.' Now wasn't the time to admit she'd never had sex, lest he think twice about this. She lifted her chin. 'I want to be your lover.'

For weeks it had been her guilty secret, but in admitting it, Charlotte felt stronger than ever before. No matter what the world said, they were simply a woman and a man caught in an utterly natural attraction. In her case, a very overdue attraction, because her early experiences of the opposite sex had left her wary and wounded.

Alessio's face drew tight. His nostrils flared, and the pulse at his temple throbbed urgently.

She'd done that. Charlotte had never realised the heady excitement of having a man want her with such intensity.

She took a step closer, but he stopped her with an abrupt gesture.

'I can't give promises except to treasure your body and give you all the pleasure I can.' Described in his low, sexy voice, that sounded absolutely perfect, yet Alessio looked grimmer than ever. 'I can offer short-term delight. But nothing else. If you're harbouring thoughts of the future—'

'Absolutely not!'

She might have fantasised about him, but Charlotte was a realist. She'd learned to face unpalatable facts early in life.

'You're the Conte Dal Lago. I'm a temporary housekeeper. Our worlds only intersect a little.' Though once upon a time, before she and her father disowned each other, she'd moved in similar circles to his, albeit in another country. But that past was dead, and she didn't regret it, because she loathed the ugliness that had been the price of staying in it. 'I have a career and long-term goals, and you have...' She floundered for a second when the only word that came to mind was *sadness*. A strange, hollow feeling opened up inside. 'Responsibilities.'

For a long moment, Alessio didn't respond, just scrutinised her as if sifting her words for truth. Then, abruptly, he inclined his head. 'I don't want to hold out false hope of a longer-term relationship.'

For a second Charlotte let herself wonder what it would be like if Alessio truly cared for her. To be loved by a man of such intensity and, she'd learned, integrity. His wife must have felt...

No, she couldn't go there.

'Nor would I. I'm leaving for Venice in a couple of months. It will be a huge career move for me, a step towards achieving my goals.'

Yet tonight she'd take a chance. Ignore the world's rules and her own and follow her instinct.

Suddenly Alessio smiled, and something inside her melted. It wasn't a carefree smile, more a twist of the lips that looked almost painful. Yet that look, and the blazing heat in his eyes, turned her knees weak.

'Then we've no time to waste.' A second later he held her in his arms, not in a waltz hold this time, but cradled up high against his chest, her long skirts trailing.

It was so sudden Charlotte was still catching her breath when he strode out of the room towards the grand staircase.

She opened her mouth to protest that he couldn't possibly want to carry her up several flights of stairs. But she didn't say a word.

His display of machismo did the strangest things

to her common sense. Instead she rested her head against his hard shoulder and relished every moment of those powerful arms sweeping her ever higher in a possessive embrace that spoke to the primitive heart of her.

'At last.' Alessio wasn't even breathing heavily as he lowered her to her feet beside the vast bed that dominated his room.

Charlotte's heart beat wildly somewhere up in her throat as she palmed the lapels of his dinner jacket, her hands a little unsteady. Because they really were going to do this. Because, against the odds, Alessio wanted *her*. It seemed remarkable, but she had no intention of pausing long enough to question her good fortune.

She wished she had more experience to draw on.

At least she had enthusiasm on her side.

'What are you smiling about?'

'Us. This.' She lifted her face to his. 'Sometimes, rarely, life can be a gift, don't you think?'

His eyes widened as if the thought had never occurred to him. Charlotte felt a pang of regret that he'd lived in the shadows of grief for so long.

Then, to her surprise, Alessio grinned. It transformed him, and she clutched at his lapels for support. What wouldn't a woman do to make him look like that every day?

'I do like gifts.' His voice was a sensual thread that wove around her, teasing erogenous zones and trailing awareness through her. This man had brought her once-dormant body out of hibernation with a vengeance. 'I especially enjoy unwrapping them.'

His fingertips skimmed the wide neckline of her dress, making her shiver and lean closer. He still hadn't kissed her. Would it be gentle and sweet or urgent?

As if reading her thoughts Alessio bent his head, but instead of touching his mouth to hers, he pressed an open-mouthed kiss to her bare shoulder. She shuddered as a tumult of sensation thundered through her. His hands slid around her back as his mouth followed the line of her bodice across to her breasts. He paused, his breath hot against her cleavage, but not as hot as the molten desire pooling low in her body.

'Alessio!' Her knees sagged, and she might have slid to the floor but for his encompassing embrace.

'Patience.' Yet there was nothing patient about his deft hand dragging the long zip down her back, then sliding the material off her shoulder and down her arm.

Cool air brushed Charlotte's skin, her back and breast, for she didn't own a strapless bra and only wore knickers beneath the dress. She felt her nipples pucker, exposed to the night air.

There was a hiss of indrawn breath, then a low, heartfelt flood of Italian that she couldn't understand. Except when she opened eyes she hadn't realised had closed, she read Alessio's expression, his reverence and delight as he cupped her breast in his warm, capable hand.

He looked as blown away as she was, and Charlotte felt a punch of triumph that indeed this wasn't one-sided. Whatever tomorrow brought when they returned to their positions as boss and employee, they were equals now.

Her eyes fluttered shut at the onslaught of profound bliss as he brought his mouth to her breast and the world fell away.

'Alessio.' It was a hoarse plea of encouragement and wonder as he took her nipple between his lips and sucked. Fiery darts zapped from her breast to her groin and back. The knees that had nearly collapsed stiffened, and she pressed closer, moving restlessly, needing contact.

He planted his feet wide, one hand splayed across her buttocks. He pulled her to stand in between his legs, bringing her into contact with that swollen ridge of masculine potency as he lifted his head.

She saw stars then. Tiny glimpses of light in those deep green eyes as if he glowed from within. Or perhaps the stars were in *her* head, products of the explosion of sensation within her.

'Charlotte.' He held her gaze as he lifted his left hand to her right shoulder and pushed the narrow velvet band down her arm. Now her other breast was exposed, yet instead of feeling hesitant, standing half naked before a man still fully dressed, she felt powerful. Because of what she saw in his expression and the throb of his erection against her belly.

Far from wanting to cover herself, Charlotte pushed her shoulders back, offering her bare breasts to him while unconsciously her lips formed into a provocative pout.

She'd never pouted in her life, or offered her body for any man's delectation. But this wasn't one-sided. She got as much pleasure revelling in Alessio's ardent response as he did from her actions.

But even more pleasure when he groaned, deep at the back of his throat and pulled her higher, drawing his tongue the length of her breast before circling her nipple and finally catching it in his teeth.

She screamed then. Not words but a strangled sound that melded desperation and delight as her body caught fire. She was aware of her fingers digging into the fine fabric at his shoulders, of the restless arch of her lower body into his and the certainty that only Alessio could satisfy this consuming craving.

'Too many clothes,' he muttered against her breast, and she agreed, reaching for his perfect bow tie.

But Alessio wasn't talking about himself. In a single movement, he shoved the heavy fabric down from her waist to her hips, from where it slid to tent around her ankles. She was so turned on that even that brush of fabric on bare skin overloaded her senses.

Charlotte swallowed hard, her tongue flicking out to moisten suddenly dry lips. She saw his heavy-lidded gaze track the movement.

'I want to eat you all up. Slowly.' His accent had thickened as his voice dropped to a sensual burr that sent a ribbon of heat straight to her sex.

'Yes!'

Restlessly she shifted her weight, trying to mould herself to his body again, but her high heels caught in her discarded dress.

Once more deft hands caught her, encircling her bare waist in a way that made her feel delicate and almost tiny against his superior size. Charlotte was fit and active and by no means weak. Yet now she was consummately aware of the profound physical differences between male and female.

She didn't even gasp when he simply lifted her off the floor, stepped over the discarded ball gown and put her down on his bed. Instead, she delighted in his strength.

Sitting on the side of the bed, wearing nothing but ivory lace knickers, while well over six feet of fully dressed, pure male magnificence towered over her, Charlotte should have felt out of her depth. Instead it felt like freedom after a lifetime of shackles.

She leaned back a little to take in the view, resting on palms planted on the bedspread that she tidied every morning. She might even have opened her knees a little wider as Alessio's hot gaze ran the length of her body. The silk and lace between her legs was wet with arousal. Could he see that?

She saw the enormous bulge in his trousers and the way his chest rose mightily as if he couldn't suck in enough air.

Yet he didn't move, and though his eyes glittered with hunger, something about the harsh twist to his lips made her wonder if he'd changed his mind.

Her confidence splintered as a chill doused her. She sat up straight and for the first time felt the urge to cover her breasts, except pride forbade that.

'Having second thoughts?' Charlotte wanted to sound understanding, but the words came out scratchy. And full of a regret she couldn't hide.

Of course he has second thoughts. He's still mourning his wife. How could you possibly think...?

'No.' His laugh was harsh and totally lacking amusement. 'I should be but, for my sins, I'm too selfish for that.'

She was torn between relief and curiosity, but before she could ask more, he spoke. 'Are *you* having second thoughts?'

She was shaking her head before he'd stopped talking. So much for pride.

'Good,' he growled. 'Because I meant what I

said, Charlotte. I want to devour you, every inch of you. I need you so badly—'

'Then stop talking and take off your clothes.'

Nerves made her voice strident, and she saw his mouth curve as speculation gleamed in his eyes. 'You like giving orders? Maybe later if you're very, very good…'

How had she ever imagined he was anything but totally in control? Just the teasing flick of one raised eyebrow and that glimmer of humour in his dark face had her shifting on the bed, trying to ease the desperate ache between her legs where the pressure built so high it felt like she might explode. If she didn't have him soon she'd go crazy.

Or maybe she was already crazy, thinking this could work. This man had been a legendary lover before his marriage. He'd expect someone experienced.

Should she tell him?

And risk rejection?

The inner debate ended the moment he ripped his bow tie off and flung it towards a chair. It slithered to the ground. So different to the neatly folded clothes he left for laundering each day.

Charlotte yanked her gaze back in time to see his gold cufflinks drop onto the bedside table. One circled and rolled off, but he didn't seem to notice, and she couldn't move to pick it up because he'd already discarded his jacket. Now he was unbuttoning his shirt. Halfway down he lost patience and tugged. She heard something tear, threads undoubtedly, but at the same time she felt something shear free within her. A last lingering thread of caution?

There was no time to follow that thought, because Alessio's hands dropped to his trousers, and her capacity for conscious thought died.

She leant forward, reaching for the tiny buckle that would undo her shoe.

'Don't! Let me do that.'

Alessio shucked his trousers, freeing himself too of socks and glossy shoes. He stood before her in nothing but black silk underwear and his own magnificence.

Charlotte felt her eyes grow round. She'd seen him shirtless. She'd seen him in rowing gear. But standing there, arms akimbo, lamplight spilling across his olive-gold skin and picking out in loving detail every line and curve of that impressive musculature, he looked like some fantasy hero made flesh. From his wide, sparely fleshed chest to his solid thighs, he was potently masculine.

Her gaze dropped to the fine line of dark hair that disappeared below the silk waistband, and instantly his erection twitched as if in response. Stunned, she met his eyes and saw his tight, rueful smile.

He lifted his shoulders. 'What can I say? I want you, Charlotte, so very, very badly.' He shook his head. '*Bad* is the operative word, isn't it? I shouldn't be doing this. I pay your wages—'

'If you say that again I'll…!'

'What will you do?' One sleek eyebrow rose as his voice turned silky. 'Punish me?'

Excitement sizzled through her. Not at the idea of punishing Alessio, but at the thought of doing with him whatever she wanted. Not that she was experienced enough to have too many ideas on that score, but with time, she'd definitely think of some.

'Stop talking, Alessio. I'm tired of waiting.'

And there it was again, that pout, that slackening of thigh muscles that spread her knees wider, that straightening of her spine that thrust her breasts towards him.

For once he didn't argue as he closed the space between them and dropped to his knees between her feet. In fact, she realised, his eyes looked a little glazed as they raked from her lips to her breasts and down to her sex.

One large hand closed around her ankle as nimble fingers plucked at the tiny buckle. Carefully, almost tenderly, he slid the sandal from her foot, then paused to press his thumbs to her instep, pushing slowly up her sole and sending lush, decadent heat pouring through her.

Charlotte bit back a moan of ecstasy.

'You like that?'

When she managed to open her eyes, it was to discover his smug expression had slipped, replaced by something raw and hungry that called to the very heart of her being.

'You can't tell?' she purred. His smile was brief as he massaged her foot again, working tired muscles and eliciting shudders of arousal. So much arousal. 'I don't think…'

Her words stopped as his lips feathered her heel, her ankle, then followed his smoothing palm up her calf. She knew about foreplay. Theoretically. She'd watched films and read books, but nothing had prepared her for Alessio focusing all that single-minded intensity on pleasing her. And he hadn't even got to the good bits.

Alessio lifted her leg higher, pressing an open-mouthed kiss to the groove behind her knee, and she shuddered as heat arced through her. Her fingers clutched the bedspread so tightly she'd probably shredded it. But the housekeeper in her, whose business it was to be concerned about such things, was nowhere to be found.

To her astonishment, Alessio propped her calf across his shoulder as he reached for her other shoe. With one leg up high, it felt natural to give in to the weight of gravity and lax muscles. She slumped back on the bed.

Her eyes drifted shut as he repeated the procedure, removing her sandal and massaging her other foot until she wondered if she might come from the sheer bliss of his touch. Kissing her slowly, deliberately, up and up her leg, building tingling anticipation in all the places he hadn't yet touched.

Her nipples pinched hard and her hips circled with need, but still Alessio made her wait.

Finally, feeling drugged with arousal, she opened her eyes to find him watching her. A dark flush coloured those high cheekbones where his flesh pulled tight. His mighty chest rose and fell, and she felt his breath hot against her thigh.

A noise escaped her throat that she'd never heard before. A protest and a plea. She wanted to reach for him so she could finally feel him inside her. Yet another part of her adored this exquisite, sensual torture.

'Are you very fond of this underwear?'

His voice was so thick it took her a second to understand his words.

She frowned. 'No, it's—'

'Good.'

Warm knuckles brushed her inner thigh. Then, in one urgent tug, he ripped the fabric free of her body.

Charlotte's mouth hung agape as ivory lace sailed through the air. She just had time to read Alessio's satisfied smile before he pressed her thighs open with those big, gentle hands and buried his face between her legs.

Her senses overloaded as he located her clitoris. His tongue circled, then stroked, and her pelvis lifted eagerly because it was impossible to stay

still. Not when each lap of his tongue sent another
bolt of lightning through her.

He traced her entrance with his finger, delving
in time with his tongue, and Charlotte gasped.

She quivered all over, pleasure rising to impossible levels as his intimate caresses breached every
expectation. How had she thought she'd understood
her body when it was clear she'd known so little
about how good it could feel? She was filled to the
brim with heat and light and a welling sensation
stronger than anything she'd ever known.

One finger became two, and she heard the slick
sound of their easy slide, felt the draw of his mouth
against her most sensitive spot.

And suddenly she was flying, racing up through
the clear, bright air, sobbing in ecstasy so powerful it edged towards fear. Till heat surrounded her,
strong arms pulling her close, and there was Alessio, his chest crushing hers, whispering reassurance in that velvety voice till the fear disappeared
and there was only rapture and this man. This one
amazing man who'd given her more than she'd ever
expected to receive.

Charlotte sobbed his name, clutching him close,
and for the first time in her life, let herself go completely.

CHAPTER TEN

WATCHING CHARLOTTE CLIMAX, holding her to him as she embraced rapture, was the most extraordinary experience. As if he shared that rapture. As if her delight were his and he'd flown to the stars with her, even though he was tight to the point of pain with unfulfilled need.

Alessio had known plenty of women and was always a gentleman about sex, ensuring his partner's pleasure before his own. Yet he couldn't recall ever feeling like this with a lover.

His arousal was torture because he'd never been so turned on in his life.

Yet gratification wasn't uppermost in his mind. Charlotte was.

He basked in the glow of knowing he'd brought her to a shattering high. But there was something more, a primal instinct that spoke of a deeper bond. She clung to him, his name a soft sigh on her lips, as she tucked herself tight against him, and part of his brain went into meltdown. At the knowledge she needed him still, even after that climax.

And at the strange jumble of emotions rampaging through him. Protectiveness, triumph, excitement and tenderness.

Alessio had never felt like this about any other woman.

Even Antonia, his dead wife.

He waited for piercing guilt to stab him. After all, this was the first time he'd been with a woman since Antonia.

Yet it didn't come.

Gently he brushed Charlotte's damp hair off her cheek, his chest squeezing as she turned her face to follow the gesture, pressing her lips to his palm and sending a shudder of exquisite pleasure arrowing to his groin.

No, it hadn't been like this with Antonia. They'd known each other for years and been friends with occasional benefits, neither looking for or expecting commitment.

Until everything changed and they'd married.

And everything went wrong.

'What are you thinking about? You look upset.'

Alessio tried to gather his thoughts. He met eyes of rich lapis lazuli, felt himself fall and keep falling. As if nothing could be better than to lose himself in those depths.

'Alessio? I'm sorry. I should have waited for you. That was selfish of me.'

Charlotte's hand fumbled between them, sliding across slick skin to hold him, and send him into one of the darkest circles of hell. Because resisting the urge to spill himself was almost impossible.

'No!' He grabbed her hand, pulling it away, wincing at the desperate effort of not coming in her hand.

The thought brought him to the edge of control, chest heaving, every muscle strung taut.

'You don't want me to touch you?' Had Charlotte's eyes always been so wide and wondering?

He shook his head. 'Of course I do, but not now.' The words emerged as a harsh growl, and he felt her delicious body stiffen, a frown corrugating her brow.

Instantly Alessio was contrite. He stroked her bottom lip with his thumb, realising they hadn't even kissed yet. There was so much he wanted to do with her, he almost didn't know where to begin.

'Because I need to be inside you when I climax, *cara*. Nothing else will do. I'm so on edge that if you touch me again, I won't be able to hold back.'

From dismay, her expression turned to delight, and he watched a rosy blush rise from her breasts to her cheeks. Almost like a woman unused to talking about sex.

Crazy how even that added to his arousal.

Face it, everything about her arouses you.

Even those damnable uniform trousers. Just as well Charlotte had no idea how perfectly they outlined her buttocks as she stretched and reached.

Which made Alessio imagine taking her from behind, pumping hard against her curvaceous rump while he found her sweet spot with his hand between her thighs.

His retreat off the bed was frantic rather than dignified, but Alessio didn't have time for smooth moves. Other than smoothing on a condom, which would be test enough of his willpower.

Fortunately he didn't disgrace himself, though his hands were shaking and his teeth tightly clenched by the time he'd put on protection. From the corner of his vision, he saw Charlotte watching him intently from under lowered lashes, and suddenly he felt as sophisticated as a schoolkid.

As if this were new. As if it wasn't something he'd done multiple times before.

Yet it felt... Alessio shook his head. He didn't have the mental capacity to work that out when every blood cell in his body was draining down to his groin.

He knelt on the bed, mouth drawing into a predatory smile as Charlotte scooted further across the bed to give them more space. He felt her eyes on him as he ran his fingers up her inner thighs, and she jumped before letting her knees loosen and open for him.

Propping himself on one hand, he stroked her sex, watching her shiver and give that eager little twist of the pelvis as if trying to follow his caress. The way she responded...

'Alessio—'

He barely caught her voice over his thundering pulse, but when he raised his gaze to hers, some of his excitement died. She gnawed her lip as if uncertain about something. About continuing?

His long-denied libido screamed denial at the

thought, but he forced himself to lift his hand from her body, nostrils flaring at the unique scent of cinnamon, sugar and female orgasm.

Razors scored his throat as he swallowed. 'What is it, Charlotte? Do you want me to stop?'

Instantly she shook her head, and relief slackened his muscles. 'No. I want you, Alessio. I just…' She heaved a shuddering sigh that made her breasts jiggle and Alessio's erection pulse. 'Nothing. Nothing at all.'

Yet there was something. He knew it. He was about to ask again when soft fingers fluttered across his shaft and he spasmed hard, on the brink.

Curiosity died, swamped by the need that had been building since she'd arrived on the island.

He caressed her sex, slipping a finger deep, then another, to be rewarded not just with slick heat, but the undulation of her hips anticipating his possession.

Suddenly he could hold back no more. Alessio settled between those pale thighs, braced himself high to save her from his full weight, and drove home in one urgent thrust.

He'd died and gone to heaven.

Ecstasy beckoned. Every sensation was perfect. Charlotte's softness. The tight velvet embrace of her body. The friction of her breasts against his heaving chest. The clamp of her hands on his shoulders and the warm stroke of her breath on his face.

Except even on the edge of losing himself, he couldn't ignore how her lax, pleasured body had stiffened. Or that tiny tugging sensation when he'd thrust, as if dislodging a barrier.

His eyes snapped open, and what he read on her face answered the question filling his mind.

Charlotte was a virgin.

Had been a virgin until seconds ago.

Her lovely mouth was pulled tight as if in discomfort, and her eyes were foggy. With pain?

Horrified, Alessio moved to withdraw.

Sharp fingernails dug into his skin, and she looped her slender leg over his as if to hold him still.

'I hurt you?' His throat was thick.

'Only for a second. And not hurt really, more...' She paused and dragged in air, making her breasts torment him as they slid against his labouring chest. 'I feel fine. More than fine.' She wrapped her other leg around his thighs, then jiggled her hips so she could encircle his buttocks with her legs. 'I want you Alessio. *Please.*'

Those words banished a rusty conscience that told him he should withdraw completely. Because he didn't mess with virgins.

She's not a virgin anymore.

It wasn't logic that convinced him, it was that pout, that sexy moue of pink lips, as if she begged for something only he could give her.

When in fact it was she giving everything to him.

The realisation sank deep into his soul, past the years of pain and isolation, to a place he hadn't known existed any longer. A place that craved warmth and connection. And Charlotte's beguiling body.

Knowing he'd have to battle his conscience and his curiosity later, Alessio gave in. He was only a man, after all, more flawed than most, and no man could resist the irresistible.

Holding her close, he rolled over so she lay above him. He watched her eyes widen and felt a tiny punch of satisfaction as her legs slid down to straddle him, and he tilted his hips, sliding deeper into welcoming heat.

'Hold on to my shoulders and sit straight.'

She was delightfully eager, and each movement sorely tested him. But it was worth it to have her seated there, taking all of him.

'Okay?' he grunted, barely leashing the need to set a driving rhythm.

'Oh, yes.' Her fingertips curled against his shoulders, digging deeper as she shifted, eyes widening at the sensation of them sliding together.

Alessio grasped her hips, urging her up. Somehow, even as he battled the compulsion to lose himself, it was Charlotte's look of wonder and delight that took centre stage.

She sank back and he thrust up, feeling her telltale shiver of response inside that made the sweat break out on his brow as he fought to go slow. Her skin flushed a deep rose, and he wanted to taste her again.

He held back. As her first lover, he had a duty to make this as good as possible for her. Yet it wasn't duty driving him. He wanted her in ecstasy even more than he needed his own release, even though it felt like waiting any longer might kill him.

Charlotte found her pace, her breaths quickening, her bright eyes holding his as he cupped and fondled her breasts, feeling the momentum build within her. Finally, as they both sped towards the inevitable peak, he gave in to his body's desperate urging and drew her down against him so they touched all the way down their bodies. He took control of their rhythm when she faltered and captured her lips with his.

Her mouth tasted as sweet as he'd imagined through all those lonely days and nights. She tasted like the promise of spring after the longest drear winter.

Restraint was impossible. Her silken hair tangled in his fingers as Alessio grabbed the back of her head and held her to him. Their lips fused as he plundered her mouth in time with the desperate plunge of their bodies.

Charlotte moaned, and he swallowed the sound.

He didn't understand how, but that felt every bit as intimate as the age-old dance of their striving bodies.

That sound, the taste of her on his tongue, the

indescribable perfection of their thrusting bodies were too much. Alessio felt the surging rush of sensation from the back of his skull to his groin, knowing he couldn't wait any longer. But then it didn't matter because at last her spasming muscles signalled her climax, drawing him tighter, milking him into ecstasy.

His last thought was to hold her safe and tight against him as they leapt together into fiery oblivion.

Alessio hugged her to him as their thundering pulses finally slowed. How long he'd lain with Charlotte in his arms he didn't know. Just that he wasn't ready to relinquish the lingering remnants of bliss.

Finally he rolled onto his side and Charlotte with him so she lay facing him, their bodies still welded together.

Her hair was in disarray, her eyes closed, and those soft lips slightly swollen from the desperate way he'd plundered her mouth. It amazed him how touching his lips to hers had undone him when he'd been able to withstand earlier temptations.

Her skin was flushed and she'd never looked more alluring.

A tiny shudder rippled down his spine.

Her eyes opened in a flash of blue, brighter than any gem in the Dal Lago treasure vault.

'Are you all right, Charlotte?'

She blinked, that sweet mouth turning up. 'More than all right. I feel fabulous.'

The stirring guilt in his gut eased. It shouldn't have been him taking her innocence and initiating her into the world of erotic delights, but he'd done no immediate harm.

With relief came a rush of other feelings. He slid his hand to her hip, shaping that delicious arc, before sliding his fingers along her silky thigh.

'You absolutely do feel fantastic.'

Another ripple of sensation, except this time in a part of his anatomy that should be completely dormant after that stunning climax. Alessio's brows twitched in a perplexed frown.

Gently but firmly, because her hands clung, he withdrew before she could realise the effect she still had on him. He needed time to think.

Alessio headed to the bathroom to dispose of the condom. But instead of lingering to get his head straight, within minutes he was back in the bedroom, drawn by a force stronger than the need to master himself.

Charlotte lay on her side in exactly the same position as when he'd left, except she cuddled a pillow to her chest. Missing him? Something shifted in Alessio's chest.

Wearing that blissed-out smile, totally naked in his bed, she was irresistible. He moved the pillow and climbed in next to her, pulling her to him.

Instantly she shaped herself against him, one

knee between his, a palm open on his chest, her other arm around his waist as she settled her head under his chin.

Alessio closed his eyes and savoured the sensation of body against body, the thrum of her heart against him, the gentle caress of her breath.

It felt peaceful. Special.

Only because you've had no physical contact with another person in over three years. This is just you relishing the comfort of an embrace.

But since when had he needed such comfort? As a kid he'd learned never to expect cuddles from absent parents intent on their pleasure-seeking lives. As an adult he enjoyed the company of lovers and friends but never *needed* anyone.

He was the one who comforted others, most notably Antonia. Though towards the end she'd avoided physical contact. His breathing stalled on acrid memories until gentle fingers smoothed along his chest as if massaging his reluctant lungs back into motion. As if Charlotte sensed his distress.

He allowed himself a moment's stillness to absorb the comfort of her touch, realising how rare it was.

How different from past experience.

Antonia had set a benchmark for him. He'd never been closer to any woman than her. Not because they'd fallen deeply in love as the world thought. The strength of their relationship had been a friendship built over years. They'd fallen into sex, becoming friends with benefits rather than soul mates. So that when the world fell apart, they'd drawn on that friendship and trust.

Not that it had been enough to save her.

'Are *you* all right, Alessio?'

He found Charlotte regarding him steadily and realised she'd quoted his own question back at him. There was something so genuine about her gaze that pierced too deep.

'Never better.' Yet her palm against his chest meant she felt his heart pounding.

Alessio didn't do vulnerable. He'd been trained from childhood to be self-sufficient and strong. So he followed a lifetime's training and took charge of the situation, changing the subject. 'Why me, Charlotte? Out of all the men you might have slept with?

No woman stayed a virgin until her midtwenties without good reason. Choosing to lose her virginity had to be a major decision.

It was only because they were so near and he watched so closely that he saw the minuscule change in her expression, the way her gaze darted away, then back again.

Despite the heat of their bodies against each other, he felt his bones frost. He knew that look.

Prevarication. Evasiveness.

She is about to lie.

Because, despite his warning earlier, she hoped for more than sex from him? That had been a problem when he was younger and not experienced enough to spell out his limits to potential lovers.

Was Charlotte hoping to tie him into a relationship?

Or perhaps use their boss-housekeeper situation and twist what had happened into something ugly, hoping for a financial settlement?

Alessio had lived in the world, and a world driven by money, long enough to know anything was possible. He'd had more than his share of avaricious women target him for what they thought they could get. Even after Antonia's death, they'd tried to push their way into his life, or at least his bed. He felt sick at the idea Charlotte might be like that.

'I could ask the same, Alessio. Why me?'

Her voice grazed his skin, a reminder that, wary as he was, she still had the capacity to undermine his willpower with the siren call of sex.

The best sex of his life.

The thought startled him. And made him yet more determined to scotch any unwanted expectations on her part.

Alessio shrugged one shoulder and raised a deliberately provocative eyebrow. 'Presumably you know my reputation. I enjoy sex. How could I resist?'

Charlotte didn't even blink. Yet he felt her shrink in his hold. Twin streaks of colour slashed her cheekbones as her expression clouded.

'You make me sound like a sweet treat that caught your eye in a shop window,' she snapped.

Her chin angled up in that familiar way she had when he'd been particularly difficult. But this time he hadn't just been difficult, but insulting. He'd hurt her.

Because he'd stepped into the unknown and it scared him!

Remorse was bitter on his tongue. Whatever Charlotte's motivation, she deserved better.

'You're right. I apologise. That made it sound like what we shared, that *you*, were a commodity. That's anything but true. Tonight was special.'

Alessio halted, trying to find a line between the truth and maintaining his pride. In the end he gave up and admitted, 'I told you in the ballroom. I've wanted you for so long. Ever since you came here.' He forced himself to go on, making the truth his penance for hurting her. 'My reputation as a lover was in the past, Charlotte. You're the first woman I've been with in years.'

CHAPTER ELEVEN

THE FIRST WOMAN in years. In years!

Charlotte stared across the water at the racing boats, adorned with fluttering flags and elaborate decorations, but didn't really take them in, instead remembering Alessio's expression as he said she'd been his first lover in years.

Since his wife?

Charlotte assumed so but hadn't liked to ask.

For despite his gentle smile, as if making up for his harsh words immediately before, there'd been a starkness in the depths of those green eyes, a seemingly infinite pain that she couldn't probe.

Not because she didn't want to—her curiosity about Alessio was deeper than the rules of politeness. But because she didn't have the heart to dredge up more hurt.

She'd seen him stiffen and turn into the stony-faced feudal lord more than once last night when some gushing female offered saccharine sympathy for his wife's death. The sympathy might have been real, but so had been the avaricious curiosity and blatant sexual interest.

Charlotte had felt jealous and protective.

Her lips twisted. Alessio didn't need her to fight his battles. Most of the night he'd used charm like a weapon, leaving eager women in his wake while steering clear of cosy chats. It was only as the evening wore on that the severe autocrat had shown through the surface gloss when people got too close.

Charlotte shouldn't have had time to notice, but no matter how she'd tried to concentrate on her hostess duties, she'd found herself fixated on Alessio.

A grunt of harsh laughter escaped. What was new?

She'd been fixated on him since the day he'd stood, blocking her way up the beach with folded arms and something curiously like dismay in that stern, beautiful face. And after what they'd shared last night, not just the amazing sex, but the unexpectedly tender way he'd held her close until she fell exhausted into sleep, that fixation was only stronger.

'What's the matter? You're not enjoying the race?'

Charlotte pivoted to see Alessio's formidable great-aunt beside her. She wore couture fashion, a scarlet pantsuit and matching suede shoes, with the panache of a woman decades younger. The light caught stunning ruby earrings that made Charlotte think instantly of Alessio.

Again.

'I'm afraid I wasn't really paying attention.'

'No doubt you have a lot on your mind.' Gleaming black eyes met hers, and Charlotte had the unnerving conviction that the other woman saw right into her head. 'With the festival and such. Last night was a triumph but a lot of work. I know my great-nephew better than to expect he exerted himself over a ball.'

It was true. Alessio had left everything to Charlotte as a punishment for daring to challenge him. Yet indignation rose at hearing his relative say so.

'Actually, Alessio has been behind the success of today's festival. He's worked incredibly hard and took the lead in planning the events.'

The old woman lifted her eyebrows. '*Alessio*, eh, not the *Conte*? And so quick to jump to his defence.'

'I—'

'No, no, don't explain. There's no need. It's a relief to see him out in the world again, not just masterminding more business success from his tower but actually *engaging* with people.'

The softening in her expression stopped the words forming on Charlotte's tongue. For it revealed a depth of feeling that surprised her. Suddenly the other woman looked her age, lines of concern obvious in her features where before Charlotte had noticed only pride and determination.

'Would you like to sit?' she said. 'There are a couple of seats free in the shade over there.'

There was a crack of husky laughter. 'Worried about the old lady standing too long, are you?' But there was warmth in her gaze as she nodded. 'Sensible of you. These legs aren't as young as they used to be, and you could probably do with the rest too. I've seen you running around all day making sure everything goes well. You'll need your strength for the dancing later.'

Charlotte was about to respond that she wouldn't be dancing, but her companion wouldn't be interested in her plans to spend the evening cleaning the ballroom. That was something she felt guilty about deferring, though she'd had no choice in it.

Because you were too busy making love to Alessio.

Having sex, she corrected herself. Love didn't enter into it.

'Just as well you found seats in the shade,' the old woman's voice interrupted. 'You look quite flushed.'

Guiltily, Charlotte met the other woman's eyes and was almost sure she read amusement there. But she couldn't know...

'Ah, here they come. The last and most important race of the day. And there's my great-nephew.'

There was no mistaking the pride in her tone, and Charlotte felt any annoyance at the other woman's perspicacity fade. Dutifully she turned to see several long rowing boats emerging from around the point. At this distance, they looked a little like Venetian gondolas with sleek lines and raised prows, but with space for several rowers.

As they drew closer, she realised the bows were

different. Each had a figurehead. Charlotte saw a lion, a mermaid, a bear and even a unicorn with a rainbow-coloured mane. There was also a rather severe saint with a halo and, streaking up past the other boats, one whose figurehead was a green dragon, breathing fire.

It was the dragon she saw everywhere in the *castello* and which always made her think of Alessio. Not just the green of his eyes but the way his initial gruffness hid such fire.

That was his boat, of course. He was easily recognisable with his broad shoulders and athletic physique, pulling at the oars with enviable strength. The boat picked up speed, scudding past first one then another of the competitors and a huge cheer rose. Her companion leaned forward, as eager as the locals.

Another boat put on a burst of speed, almost matching Alessio's, and another group cheered rowdily.

All around people jumped to their feet, barracking for their favourite boat. Charlotte's heart was in her mouth as she urged Alessio's boat on, which was crazy because it was just a boat race. But something deeper than logic made her hope he'd win.

Because she wanted to see him smile?

Because he deserved something to celebrate after what she guessed were years of grief? Yet

Charlotte thought Alessio would hate being the object of her sympathy.

When his boat sped across the winning line first, she was on her feet like the woman beside her.

A gnarled hand grasped hers. 'There. He always was a superb rower.' Then, as if suddenly aware that she'd grabbed Charlotte's hand, she moved back, and when she spoke again her voice was cool. 'I'm glad it was a team of islanders who won. No doubt he had the whole crew practising hard each morning.'

'He did. Morning and evening.'

'He always did take things seriously. When he commits to something there's no turning back.'

Yet she didn't make that sound like a positive thing.

The older woman sighed and slanted her an assessing look before saying softly, 'His wife died here, in the lake, you know. He didn't row for at least a year after that. Wouldn't go out on the water or swim. It's such a relief to see him active again.'

Charlotte stared, hearing the emotion in her companion's voice and seeing a bright glint that might even have been tears in those dark eyes. Her heart ached for Alessio, so grief-stricken by his wife's death, and for this old lady who clearly cared so much.

He wasn't the ogre he sometimes went out of his way to appear. Charlotte was more and more convinced that Alessio felt too much. He was a proud man battling demons by locking himself away with his grief.

Something deep inside her chest twisted savagely.

How much he must have loved his wife.

Charlotte had no experience of such love. Her father had viewed her mother's death is inconvenient rather than a tragedy. She'd grown up convinced that romantic love was a fantasy spruiked by poets and playwrights.

'Silly boy,' the old lady murmured. 'As if he'd have been able to stop her drowning even if he'd been here.'

Charlotte frowned. That didn't make sense. If Alessio had been here, surely he'd have been able to prevent the accident that took his wife's life? He was so confident on the water, she suspected he was a powerful swimmer.

She was about to ask for clarification when the other woman urged her down into the crowd to watch the victorious team come ashore, and the opportunity disappeared.

The incomers had all left the island and the sun had set when Alessio finally had an opportunity to be with Charlotte. All day there'd been so much to do, not just as the festival's official host, but as one of the islanders, participating like everyone else in the activities.

It had been a strain at times, but he'd found it

strangely therapeutic, plunging back into the life of the island on the most raucous day of the year.

He'd caught Beatrice watching him more than once, a satisfied look on her lined face, but to her credit, she hadn't said 'I told you so' despite three years of nagging, trying to draw him out into the world again.

The trouble was that, while today had been satisfying, he still carried the terrible burden of guilt that nothing could erase.

Except being with Charlotte last night. You didn't feel guilty then. You felt alive in a way you hadn't done for years, even before you married Antonia.

The hairs on the back of his neck prickled. He told himself it was with shame that he should feel so much for a woman he hardly knew.

Yet it felt like he knew her. Not all the details of her family or her past, but at some visceral level, deeper than words.

He looked across the cobbled square, strung with lights and filled with islanders in colourful, festive clothes, dancing to live music. He located her easily. All day he'd been able to sense unerringly where she was, no matter how thick the crowd.

Alessio's belly tightened as something rose inside him. Desire, yes, but more too. Need? Possessiveness? Relief?

She danced with Mario's ne'er-do-well greatnephew, her golden hair flying free around her shoulders as her red summer dress flared around her legs.

Charlotte looked fresh and pretty in that casual dress. The first sight of her in it this morning had dried Alessio's mouth. He'd wanted to hustle her back to his room and lock the door to keep her to himself.

But he'd had obligations, and she'd been looking forward to the festivities.

Who is this woman?

She seemed equally at home acting as chatelaine in a castle as mixing with this tight-knit community. She took Beatrice in stride, mixed easily with Europe's elite yet had been a sexual innocent. She had the backbone to stand up to Alessio, yet at other times she fitted perfectly into the role of discreet housekeeper.

He'd seen the appreciative and speculative looks she'd received last night. No doubt having her as his hostess would ignite a whole new round of gossip, but Alessio didn't care what the world thought. He was too busy puzzling her out for himself.

That English banker last night had recognised her, not as a housekeeper at a Swiss hotel, but as a guest at exclusive society events in Britain.

Alessio had been determined to get to the bottom of that last night and demand answers from her. But when he'd farewelled the last of his guests and turned to Charlotte, he'd been sidetracked by need.

And it hadn't dimmed. Last night had been intense, but if he'd hoped it would cure him of this burning hunger, he'd been mistaken. His need had merely intensified.

Alessio shouldered his way through the dancers as the music died. He'd done his duty, dancing at this final event just for locals with everyone from eighty-year-old Rosetta to fourteen-year-old Sonia. Now it was *his* turn.

As arranged with the band, the final tune of the night was a slow number. He reached for Charlotte. 'My dance,' he growled.

Her young partner read Alessio's expression and melted away.

'You scared him off.' Her gaze challenged him, yet she moved eagerly into his embrace. Alessio felt himself finally relax.

'He'll get over it.' Alessio didn't have sympathy to spare, not when he'd spent the whole day bereft of Charlotte in his arms.

Years of celibacy—that had to be the reason for this craving.

Yet he wasn't sure the explanation was so simple.

He pulled her to him, uncaring of curious eyes, knowing that he needed these moments with her pressed close, her body moving with his. A reward for all he'd endured, facing the public again, pretending all was right in his world.

Except he discovered to his surprise that things hadn't been as onerous as expected. He'd enjoyed a lot of today. Especially when he'd looked up and caught Charlotte smiling at him and felt anticipation sear through him.

'You've enjoyed yourself?'

Her smile was wide and unstinting, hitting Alessio's chest like a shaft of sunlight. 'Absolutely. It's been marvellous. The music, the people, the food. Congratulations on winning the boat race, by the way. That was impressive.'

He shrugged and held her closer. 'We had a good team.'

'Today's market seemed successful too, don't you think?'

'It was. Very.' He paused. 'Thank you, Charlotte. It mightn't always seem like it, but I appreciate what you've done here. Making me see what I should have noticed long before.'

She shook her head. '*You're* the one who's made the difference. You're the one who got the festival off the ground.'

Only because she'd forced him out of his eyrie and back into his community.

The music ended to applause and cheers, and Alessio forced himself to release Charlotte. He turned in response to calls for a speech and found his fingers tangling with hers. He tightened his grip for an instant before forcing himself to let go. But the touch of her hand stayed with him as he closed the festival. He didn't rush, acknowledging everyone involved while nodding and smiling in response to the crowd's thanks.

They deserved thanks too for their understanding and forbearance over the last couple of years. He might have been in a dark place, but he'd had no right to curtail their celebrations. Seeing them all in holiday mode today had brought home to him in stark clarity how self-absorbed he'd been.

'You're very quiet.' Charlotte said as they approached the *castello* together, a careful arm's length apart.

Alessio turned and caught her expression. Reserved. Impenetrable. Like when she'd been simply his housekeeper. As if they'd never been intimate. As if she hadn't given him her virginity and more besides. It felt like she'd ignited a light in the darkness of his soul that, once lit, still glowed brightly.

The idea of her retreating appalled him. Last night had changed things in so many ways, and despite the complications that brought, he couldn't wish it undone. For good or ill, they'd embarked on an affair, and he wasn't ready for it to end.

'It's been an eventful day.'

Alessio pushed open the big door and gestured for her to precede him. Once inside he bolted it, feeling a stab of satisfaction that finally they were alone.

But when he turned, Charlotte had moved away, not quite meeting his eyes as she spoke. 'I suppose I'd better make a start on the ballroom.'

'Because it bothers your efficient heart to think of it not gleaming?' He paced towards her, watching her eyes widen as they locked on his. 'Do you have a secret cleaning fetish? Or is it an excuse to avoid being alone with me?'

He stopped before her, reading her answer in her face. She was unsure of herself, and suddenly Alessio was remembering how it had felt last night as her first lover.

A carnal shudder ran down his spine and shot through his belly to his groin. He knew now that this sparking heat between them was new to her. For that matter, it felt unique to him.

'I want you, Charlotte. Still. More.' His voice was a rumbling note deep in his chest. 'Last night wasn't enough for me. But if you don't feel the same, I won't pester you—'

'No! It's not that.' She planted one hand over his quick-thudding heart. 'I wondered if last night was a one-off and today we'd return to our normal lives. We agreed to something brief.'

'Brief, yes, but not that brief.' The idea of not having her again was impossible.

She surveyed him solemnly, her expression at odds with the way she leaned in, and it took everything he had not to sweep her into his arms.

'It's your decision, Charlotte.' He still had some scruples left.

'So you won't object if I walk away.' He stifled

a groan. He'd been so sure she wanted him still. 'My head says I should,' she whispered, 'but...'

She moved then, lifting her mouth to his. Instantly he hauled her close. Lightning sheeted through him. His blood sizzled, and the erection stretching his trousers was instantaneous as their bodies pressed and all that feminine softness strained against him.

But more than that was the wave of relief that engulfed him. Alessio had waited all day for this. Even pulling at the oars of a racing boat or welcoming dignitaries to the events, at least half his mind had been on Charlotte and the need to hold her, have her.

He slid his fingers through her silky hair, cradling the back of her skull as he leaned into the kiss. She opened her mouth eagerly, drawing him in and stroking her tongue against his with barely a hint of the sweet clumsiness that had intrigued him last night. As if it wasn't just sex but kissing that was new.

That thought finally made him break the kiss. Though he almost changed his mind at the way Charlotte lifted her head to follow his mouth with hers. Heat doused him and his hands shook as he gently held her away. This woman undid him so easily.

All the more reason to set some ground rules.

She pouted up at him, almost undoing his resolve. 'Alessio?'

'Soon, *cara*.' He couldn't resist stroking that sensuous bottom lip with his thumb, pressing it open and then swooping down for another kiss, swift but ravaging. He heard her tiny moan, and it sent a thrill of temptation winding through his body till he almost forgot his good intentions. It was only as he felt his hands shaping her buttocks, lifting her off her feet and up against his erection, that he realised what he was doing.

Rather than release her, Alessio compromised, wrapping her close and carrying her into the nearest room. It was a formal salon, antique furniture upholstered in pale green silk. He walked stiff-legged across the honey-coloured parquetry and lowered her, centimetre by delectable centimetre, down his throbbing body.

Someone gasped. Her hands clutched, and he gave in. Instead of sitting beside her on the long lounge, he sank onto it and drew her onto his lap, his arm around her back, her breast snug against his chest.

'We need to talk,' he said.

Talking was the last thing he wanted.

'Go on.'

'I need to know exactly what you want, Charlotte.' He needed to be sure she didn't feel pressured.

A smile he could only describe as lascivious unfurled across those pink lips and made his erection pulse against her buttocks. Her eyes rounded in shock, amusing him but at the same time damping his arousal. Because it was a reminder of her inexperience against his.

Was he taking advantage?

Alessio loosened his arms, but it was beyond him to move away. He wasn't a saint. He was a sinner through and through. Despite her inexperience, despite being her employer, he craved her with every particle of his newly awakened libido.

A shadow passed over his heart as he looked into Charlotte's clear, questioning eyes. What was he doing, even thinking of an affair with her?

'What do I want? That's easy,' she said in a husky voice that twisted his gut inside out. 'I want *you*, Alessio. I want more of what we did last night.'

A delicate blush coloured her cheeks, but her look was direct.

Alessio shut his eyes, a prayer of thanks forming in his head when he couldn't remember the last time he'd prayed.

'I think we can arrange that.' As if he wasn't already fighting the need to ravish her out of that red dress and lose himself in her sweet body. Heat drenched his skin as he imagined it.

'But we need to set some boundaries,' Charlotte said, dragging him back from his eager thoughts.

He inclined his head. 'I agree.'

'You first,' Charlotte said. Her tongue cleaved to the roof of her mouth at the way he devoured her with his eyes, but this was important, and she strove to concentrate even as she shifted on his lap, relishing the feel of his rigid shaft beneath her buttocks. Had she really taken all that length inside her last night? The thought made the muscles inside clench needily. 'What boundaries?'

'I told you I can only offer sexual pleasure.'

She nodded, biting off the impulse to admit he'd done that to perfection.

He didn't need her gushing about his sexual prowess. He knew the effect he had on her.

'I want more than a single night.' His voice ground deliciously low, and she felt her nipples peak in response. 'I want an affair.' Sea-green eyes held hers, and she wanted to dive into those depths and lose herself in the tide of passion rising through her body. 'But I can't offer more than that.' He frowned down at her as if to make sure she heard every word. 'Not *won't* but *can't*, Charlotte. That's never going to be an option.'

Because he's still in love with his dead wife. Hadn't his great-aunt said as much?

Charlotte had known it, yet having it spelled out made some fragile, barely formed hope sink like a pebble tossed into deep water.

'But I don't want to take advantage of you. If you don't want that, I promise not to touch you again.'

The jut of his clenched jaw and his febrile gaze told her that while Alessio would be as good as his word, it would be difficult for him. Silly how wonderful that made her feel. 'Or if you prefer to leave now, I'll write you a glowing reference for the work you've already done, and not stand in your way.'

'So,' she said slowly, moistening dry lips and feeling heat explode in her pelvis at the way his eyes followed the movement. 'My choices are hot sex with you for however long this attraction lasts. Maybe a week or—'

'Months.' His voice, thick with desire, made her feel more confident. 'It will take a while to satiate this.'

'Or I could get up and walk away now and never have you touch me again.'

Appalling how desperate that made her feel. She could no more turn her back on Alessio than she could scale the Matterhorn.

'Guess which I choose.' She lost herself in those mesmerising eyes. 'I want more too. I've got a lot to learn, and you're just the man to teach me.'

The subtle shift in his expression, the flare of aristocratic nostrils and the softening of his taut mouth, told her he wanted this as much as she did.

'But I have my own plans, and they don't include being known as a rich man's mistress.' She felt him stiffen, his eyes turning unfathomable. 'My reputation is important to me. I can't have it damaged by gossip that I'm sleeping with my employer.' No matter how much she wanted Alessio. 'Acting as your hostess last night probably already set tongues wagging.'

'You're right. I'm sorry.' Concern furrowed his brow. 'I'll do what I can to scotch any rumours. As for our relationship, I'll take every precaution to keep it private. There'll be no more dancing together at local fêtes.'

Charlotte felt a pang of loss. How wonderful it would be simply to enjoy this extraordinary attraction. To be carefree, not fretting over what others thought or where this might lead.

But it couldn't lead anywhere.

She sat straighter. 'Venice is calling, and I'm not looking for a long-term partner.'

Work had been her salvation and she clung to its security—the only security she'd known since her mother died. Her goal was to run her own upmarket guest house. Working in other people's hotels wasn't enough. She wanted to use the hostessing skills she'd learned from her mother to create a warm, intimate atmosphere in her own home that guests would come back for again and again.

'That makes you different to most women I know.' He paused, his look searching. 'Did something bad happen, Charlotte? Something that put you off sex?'

She blinked, stunned at his perspicacity. No one else had picked up on her reserve around intimacy.

No one else knew you were a virgin until last night. Strange how with Alessio, she'd been anything but reserved.

'Nothing I couldn't cope with.' It was only half

a lie, but she didn't want to talk about it. She'd got away with a torn dress and badly shaken nerves. And a mistrust she'd never lost. 'Other than meeting too many men out for what they can get, who don't care who they trample in the process.' She met his arrested stare and hurried on. 'I didn't mean—'

'It's okay, Charlotte. I understand.' Another pause as he surveyed her intently. 'A guest last night recognised you, said he'd met you at a spectacular party in an English mansion. But you weren't working. You were one of the guests.'

Instinctively Charlotte pulled away, except his strong arm still encircled her. 'You think I'm some imposter?'

His gaze pinioned her. 'I simply think there's a lot more to you than you let on. Last night you fitted in as if you'd attended balls for years. Don't tell me it's because you're used to meeting guests. It was more than that.'

Charlotte's skin prickled. She had nothing to hide, yet it felt like she'd been caught out in a lie. 'My parents were wealthy,' she said eventually, 'and they liked to entertain. I attended a lot of formal events.'

'They're dead? My condolences.'

'My mother died, but my father's very much alive.' She lifted tight shoulders. 'We're not in contact.' Still Alessio regarded her. 'I don't want to talk about him.'

'Okay.' Alessio pulled her close, and suddenly thoughts of her father and the past fled as she responded to the promise of his virile body. He planted his palm on her thigh and heat drenched her, moisture blooming at her feminine core. 'I'm sure we can find other things to discuss.'

Instantly unhappy memories were replaced by urgent physical need. Charlotte embraced it eagerly. Never had she known anything so perfect as being with Alessio.

In some distant part of her mind, a warning clanged, but then Alessio's hand slid under her dress to inch up her thigh, and caution died as bliss beckoned.

CHAPTER TWELVE

BEYOND ALESSIO'S BROAD SHOULDERS, she caught the pink glow of dawn streaming into his room. But then he moved down her body, peppering a line of kisses from her breast to her navel, across to her hip, before sinking between her open thighs.

Charlotte gasped, body arching, electrified by the devastating touch of his tongue. They'd been lovers nearly a month, and he still made her feel like it was the first time again with all its wonder and power.

She trembled as he settled deeper, one hand beneath her bottom, lifting her into his caress, the other splayed across her thigh in what felt to her bemused brain like possessiveness.

Like the way, even in sleep, he anchored her to him.

Like the gleaming look in his eye every time she emerged from a swim to find him waiting on the beach with her towel, ready to rub her dry before carrying her indoors to the nearest sofa and having his wicked way with her.

Wicked, that's what it was, to make a woman so blissed out she couldn't think.

He'd indolently lean against the doorjamb, watching her make the bed, then saunter over and tumble her onto it, saying he was so turned on from watching her he couldn't resist.

She loved it all. Loved *this*. The rising tide of excitement as her body thundered towards fulfilment, the feel of his silky hair in her clutching hands and his abrasive morning stubble against her inner thighs. How his eyes held hers, watching her tumble towards ecstasy.

Charlotte shuddered, overcome by the enormity of it all. And the need not to be alone as he drove her to climax.

'Alessio!' It was a gasp so hoarse she wasn't sure the sound registered. 'I need you with me.'

He rose on hands and knees, prowling up her body, a magnificent predator. Except his eyes held something more than sexual hunger.

As he closed the gap between them, blocking the dawn light with his broad shoulders, her throat clogged. She had no name for the expression he wore, yet it filled her with something profound. Tenderness, a sense of belonging and connection at the deepest level.

Her heart rolled over.

'Charlotte.' He made her name sound like a welcome and a prayer as she opened her arms, drawing him down.

This was what she adored above everything else. His weight on her. The oneness as he sank into her. She was so aroused physically but also emotionally. This felt…

She squeezed her eyes shut, fighting the hot prickle of tears that had nothing to do with pain or distress but came from being completely overwhelmed.

A calloused palm cupped her cheek. Alessio's warm breath on her face was a benediction. '*Cara*, look at me.'

She did, seeing the familiar excitement melded with an affection that echoed her feelings.

'I'm all right,' she whispered before he could question her. 'Just a little…overwhelmed. I need you, Alessio.'

She wrapped her arms around him, one hand on his taut buttock, the other around the satiny, hot skin of his back.

Better that he think her response purely physical than guess her tangled emotions.

'It's okay.' Slowly he moved, thrusting deep and creating a heavenly symphony of delight. 'I've got you, *tesoro*. I'll look after you.'

Her smile was wobbly, and then it disappeared altogether as their bodies quickened, taking up that now familiar, triumphant tempo that led them both into bliss. They stayed wrapped in each other's arms, riding out the wonder of it, locked together as if nothing could ever separate them.

Even when it was over, neither moved. Their hearts thundered in tandem, their desperate breaths in sync, sharing shudders of ecstasy as they came back to the real world together.

Except the real world had changed, she realised.

Nothing would ever be the same.

It changed the moment you met him.

The moment you gave yourself to him.

The moment you fell for him.

Charlotte closed her eyes, as if that way she could avoid the truth. But she was in Alessio's arms, tucked close, her favourite place in the world.

She breathed deep, inhaling the spicy scent that she'd associate with him forever. Warm, male skin, cedarwood and something exotic like frankincense. And the primal scent of sex.

Except in her case she feared it wasn't mere sex. It was love.

She'd never expected that to happen. Not after seeing her parents' unhappy marriage and the way so many men treated women as disposable assets, available for their convenience.

Yet although Alessio had made it abundantly clear this could only be a short-term liaison, he'd given her far more than she expected. The sex was brilliant, energising, satisfying, addictive. At the same time he gave her respect and consideration. Plus his tenderness was beyond price.

Far from being an ogre or uncaring playboy, she suspected this man had a heart bigger than he let on. He was caring and thoughtful but seemed determined not to let anyone, apart from those on the island who'd known him forever, realise it.

Because he'd been hurt. Was still hurting.

She wanted to heal him.

She didn't want to leave in another month. She had a horrible feeling it might break her heart.

How had it come to this?

Yearning for the impossible, for a man still in love with his dead wife.

A sound of distress escaped, and instantly he stroked her hair. 'Charlotte?'

She gathered herself and opened her eyes, forcing a smile. 'You're a little heavy.' He wasn't. His body covering hers was bliss, but it was the only excuse she could think of.

Instantly he rolled onto his side, hugging her close. 'Sorry. I should have moved.' He paused. 'Are you sure you're all right?'

There it was again. Concern. An awareness of her emotions that she'd never encountered in anyone else. She needed to change the subject because she couldn't talk about her feelings. She was too churned up.

'I've never been better.'

She slanted him what she hoped was a mischievous smile though she couldn't meet his eyes. Quickly she looked away, hoping for inspiration. Her gaze landed on a small, very old painting that had fascinated her from the moment she saw it. Like the one downstairs, it showed a creature that looked like a cross between a dragon and a sea serpent, its coiling tail encircling a beautiful woman.

'What is it with your family and dragons, Alessio? I know there was supposed to be a local monster, but they're everywhere in the *castello*.'

He shifted as if settling more comfortably. 'You don't know the story?' He stroked her hair, and some of her tension eased. She shook her head.

'My family have dominated this region for centuries, so long that they've come to represent the place. Legend is that there was a monster in the lake, and the people would appease it by giving it something precious every year. One year instead of the best fruits of the harvest or gold and jewels, for some reason they offered a beautiful blonde virgin. They left her on this island for the monster to take.'

Charlotte shuddered. 'I don't like this story.'

A laugh rumbled up from his chest beneath her ear. 'Don't worry, it ends well. The official version is that a saint saved her by killing the monster and setting her free. There's a monastery dedicated to him on an island at the far end of the lake.

'But the *real* story is told by the locals. They say the dragon was actually the Conte Dal Lago, the rapacious baron who ruled with an iron fist and took whatever he wanted. Until he met his match, in the form of a golden-haired virgin.'

Charlotte's eyes met Alessio's.

Stupid, the way her heart leapt. At the weird coincidence that she was blonde and had been a virgin when they met. And because part of her yearned for the Conte Dal Lago to claim her as his, not for a brief affair, but for life.

Because you want Alessio more than you've ever wanted anything.

More than the career that had been her salvation when she'd lost her mother and cut herself adrift from her father. More than the independence she'd thought her greatest asset.

But life was no fairy tale.

'It doesn't sound like a match made in heaven. If he were used to taking whatever he wanted, he probably grew tired of her once the novelty wore off. And she didn't have much choice in it, did she?' She gave Alessio a smile she hoped was coolly amused. 'Just as well it's a myth.'

Alessio frowned, not sharing her brittle amusement. He regarded her intently as if seeing something in her expression that she'd hoped wasn't there.

Charlotte turned towards the bright daylight streaming through the windows. 'It's later than I thought. I need to shower and get moving.'

She leaned across and pressed her lips to his, savouring his welcoming kiss, knowing this was a short-term privilege that would end all too soon.

When she pulled away, she avoided his eyes. 'If you don't mind, I won't join you for breakfast. I have to meet some suppliers.'

She was out of the bed before he could answer, hurrying towards the bathroom.

Which meant she didn't see Alessio's assessing look.

Charlotte had been like a cat on hot bricks all day.

Whenever Alessio tracked her down, it was to

discover her bustling off to some new task. At first he'd thought she was disturbed by the continued speculation about her in the media. The world seemed fascinated by his mysterious, glamorous hostess. When he'd mentioned that, she'd shrugged it off. Yet it felt like she avoided him, always with a good excuse.

Alessio was edgy. Something had happened this morning. Something that felt like an invisible wedge driven between them. He'd seen and felt her withdrawal even as he held her in his arms.

It had been…disquieting.

Even if his saner self said that was a good thing. Better that Charlotte didn't grow comfortable in this relationship.

Because it had to end.

Strangely, instead of bringing relief, the thought made Alessio's gut spasm.

As if he didn't like the idea of Charlotte leaving.

He wasn't ready for her to withdraw, much less leave. The suspicion that *she'd* have no regrets about going unsettled him.

Which was why midafternoon found him searching for her, only to pull up short, his heart beating a sickening rhythm when he discovered where she was.

Alessio stopped in the doorway of the sunny room, stiff fingers clutching the doorjamb, stomach churning.

'Alessio!'

She put down a duster and smiled. But only for an instant because then he saw it again—her withdrawal—as if she put up an invisible barrier.

Something sour exploded on his tongue. Disappointment? Loss?

'What are you doing in here?' Her eyes widened at his brusque tone, and he tried to temper it. 'There's no need to clean here. The room's not used.'

The empty nursery mocked him. He hadn't been here in three years. The sight of it unleashed regret and pain.

He watched Charlotte's gaze travel from the picture books that had never been read to the pristine cot and the rocking chair where he'd last seen Antonia, curled up in a ball of misery.

He drew a shuddering breath, fighting memories.

'I'm sorry, Alessio.' Charlotte approached him, regret and understanding in her eyes as she reached for him. 'This must be hard for you. I—'

He jerked his arm away. 'You think I need your sympathy?' His voice was sharp like the brittle darkness inside him. It was easier to lash out than let himself think. 'You presume too much!'

He stepped back, dropping his arm from the doorjamb, but the miasma followed, clouding his thoughts and tainting the air. When it cleared, Alessio saw she'd paled, her body rigid.

The churning in his belly intensified, but this

time with self-disgust. 'Charlotte…' He crossed the threshold, but she recoiled and he slammed to a stop.

It wasn't just shock in her eyes—it was hurt. He'd wounded her because she'd glimpsed his pain and regret. And because, after the happiness they'd shared, the sudden bleak memories felt overwhelming.

What did that make him? When had he become a man who'd hurt someone whose only crime was to care? Not just anybody, but his lover. A woman who brought him pleasure and a measure of peace and joy he'd never expected to experience again.

His heart slammed against his ribs and shame thickened his throat. 'I'm sorry, Charlotte. You didn't deserve that.' Still she stood, unmoving and wary. Alessio almost wished she'd berate him. Her silent appraisal scoured him to the bone. 'I've hurt you, and I'd do anything I could to undo that.'

He drew a breath and found himself saying something totally unexpected. 'Can we go somewhere and talk about it?'

Eventually she nodded, and he led her to a window seat at the end of the corridor looking out over the lake. He waited till she was seated beside him, ankles crossed primly and hands clasped in her lap, but he read the tension in her narrow shoulders. He wanted to hug her to him for his own sake as well as hers, but he didn't have the right after the way he'd ripped up at her.

Alessio scraped his hand around the back of his neck, trying to ease rigid muscles. 'You're right. It was hard, being in the nursery. I haven't gone through that door in three years. I should be thanking you for noticing and caring, not attacking you.' He met her dark blue gaze and let the truth out. 'I've got in the habit of pushing people away, especially sympathetic ones.' He shrugged. 'In the past most of them had an agenda, to get the gory details of my marriage to share with others or to insinuate themselves into my life for their own ends.'

It was amazing how blatant some women had been, offering physical intimacy supposedly to ease his wounded heart. But he'd read the avaricious glitter in their eyes.

'You don't think I...?'

'No!' He covered her hands with one of his and felt something inside him ease when she didn't pull away. 'Not for a second. That's why my reaction was unfair. I knew you saw my pain, and that made me feel...vulnerable.' His mouth curled in a tight smile. 'I've spent years telling myself I don't do vulnerable.'

'So you attacked instead.' Her voice was unreadable.

'I'm appalled, because I know you genuinely care. You've got no hidden agenda, and I know how rare that is.' Maybe that's why this affair felt different to anything he'd experienced. 'Obviously you've guessed some of what happened.'

Her fingers twitched beneath his, but she didn't pull away, and he felt himself relax a little. Charlotte was, he realised, the first person he'd reached for, emotionally or physically, in a long, long time.

'You and your wife hoped to have a child.'

'Antonia, my wife was Antonia.' How long since he'd spoken her name aloud? 'She spent so much time and effort designing the nursery. It had to be perfect.' And it gave her a distraction from other things.

Alessio looked at his hand joined with Charlotte's, fascinated that such a simple touch should feel so good. He met her eyes and read understanding and sincerity. He could trust her not to share his secrets.

'We weren't just hoping for a baby. Antonia was pregnant.' He felt Charlotte's jolt of surprise. 'That's why we married.'

'I see,' she said carefully.

No, she didn't, but it was enough to explain about the baby without discussing his marriage.

He and Antonia had been friends for years and occasional lovers, but as soon as she found herself pregnant, both had wanted to bring up their child as part of a family. Both had wanted to be better parents than theirs had been.

'We left Rome and settled here because it was quieter.' That was true as far as it went. For a second, Alessio contemplated blurting out the whole story to Charlotte. But he wouldn't burden her with that.

Her hand turned in his, squeezing. 'It would be a great place to bring up a child.'

Alessio shrugged. 'We hoped so. My memories of growing up here are mixed. My parents were the absentee type, but I loved the lake and the people here.' He paused. 'But it's academic. The baby died. Antonia miscarried.'

Charlotte covered his hand now with hers, her touch solid and comforting. 'I'm so sorry.'

Just that. Nothing about trying to imagine how he'd felt or some platitude about time healing. Yet Alessio felt his wound-too-tight grief ease just a little. Grief for their unborn child and for Antonia. Even for himself.

'Thank you,' he said eventually, his tongue thick. 'I haven't talked about it. Only a few people knew...'

'I won't tell anyone.'

That's not what he'd meant. It had been a simple statement of fact. Maybe Beatrice was right and he should have found a grief counsellor. Alessio couldn't imagine discussing his private life, and Antonia's, with a paid stranger.

Yet talking with Charlotte felt natural.

'Thank you.' He squeezed her hands, then withdrew his. It wouldn't do to grow too accustomed to her ready sympathy. Though it was harder than expected to pull away. 'My anger in the nursery was misdirected. I—'

'It's okay, Alessio. I think I understand. You were hurting, and you lashed out.'

'You make me sound like a toddler having a tantrum.'

Her mouth curved in a crooked, tender smile that shot a dart of longing right through him. Not longing for sex but for Charlotte in his arms, making him feel as if, for once, things would be all right.

Hell! He *was* like a needy child. Maybe the toddler analogy was right.

'We all have our moments.'

He met her understanding look and wondered about Charlotte's emotional moments.

She was remarkably poised, with a sangfroid many public figures would envy. It was only when they made love, or danced, or laughed together, that she revealed the warm, vivacious woman he'd always suspected lurked behind the professional image. She was so contained, rarely giving a hint about her past. Curiosity consumed him. He needed to *know* Charlotte in more than the carnal sense.

It was something he'd never felt about any previous lover except Antonia. But that was because they'd agreed to share their lives. Yet his feelings for Charlotte weren't like what he'd felt for his wife.

Thankfully. He'd never marry again. He shuddered, remembering the fraught drama of it all. The loss of control. The never-ending guilt.

It was definitely time to change the subject. He'd satisfied Charlotte's curiosity. Now it was her turn.

Unable to resist any longer, he reached for her hand, threading his fingers through hers, enjoying the way they fitted together despite their differing sizes.

'Tell me something important about yourself, Charlotte. Something from your past.'

'Because you shared a secret with me?'

Alessio met her steady look. 'No. Because I want to understand you.'

There it was again, the feeling that Alessio *saw* her. That she *mattered*.

It was tempting to read too much into that. The reality was probably that Alessio was uncomfortable talking about his painful past and wanted to change the subject. Yet as their gazes meshed, it didn't feel like that.

What did she have to lose? It wasn't as if she had a guilty secret. 'What you want to know?'

'Tell me about your family, about your father.'

She must've flinched, for Alessio gently squeezed her hand. 'You go straight for the jugular, don't you? No wonder you're so successful in business.'

'The last thing I want is to hurt you, Charlotte. But I suspect I'm not the only one who might benefit from a listening ear.'

Was it that obvious? Charlotte had thought she'd done an excellent job of getting over her past.

Except she'd let it colour so much of her life. She hadn't returned to England in all these years. She'd never dated, much less taken a lover until Alessio. She'd never trusted a man enough to let him into her life.

At least with Alessio she knew he wasn't scheming for anything apart from her body. She admired his honesty even if she found herself wanting more.

Yet he was grieving for his wife and child. She couldn't expect more from him. He might have married Antonia for their baby, but he was so distraught it was clear he'd fallen in love with her. Her heart squeezed, remembering his expression of stark loss.

Charlotte curled her fingers around his, drawing strength. 'There's not much to tell. I adored my mother and despised my father. I haven't seen him since she died.'

'Do you miss home?'

The sharp, hollowing sensation in her chest was instantaneous. 'I miss the home I used to have, but it doesn't exist any more.'

'It's been sold?'

She met his concerned stare and felt annoyed with herself. The man had just spoken of the most intimate personal tragedy. Her past was nowhere near as traumatic, yet here she was, hoarding her misery as if it were unique.

'No.' She gathered her thoughts. 'My mother

was the last of an aristocratic family and lived on a country estate. She was on the point of selling up when she married my father. He was a businessman with pretensions to grandeur. Acquiring a country pile where he could entertain distinguished guests with an aristocratic hostess helped him climb the social ladder. As for my mother, she'd been desperate to save the estate not just for herself but for the tenants and employees. My father's money accomplished that.'

Alessio nodded.

'Most of my childhood I was happy. I loved the estate and my mother, and my father was away a lot.'

'We have that in common. I rarely saw my parents.' Another revelation from Alessio. What had happened to the taciturn man she'd first met? 'Sorry. I shouldn't have interrupted. Go on.'

'There's not much to tell. My father is a bombastic bully. He demanded absolute obedience from everyone, and if he didn't get it instantly, you paid dearly.'

Alessio's voice was sharp. 'He was violent?'

'Not physically. He had other ways of hurting people.' Though the last time she'd seen him, he'd been so apoplectic with rage she'd half-expected physical assault. 'My mother ran a stable. One day I badly disappointed my father.' It was something she'd done often, not getting the right marks in school, not making friends with the right people, not being nice enough to his slimy friends. 'The next day when she went there, she discovered her horses gone. They'd been packed up in the night to be sold without her knowledge. She'd bred some of them herself.' It had almost broken her heart, and Charlotte had been distraught with guilt.

Alessio muttered something in Italian that sounded like a curse. 'He controlled you through your mother?'

'And vice versa. My mother put up with a lot for my sake.' Too much. 'Then, suddenly she died. One day she was fine, and the next she had an aneurysm and died instantly.'

'I'm sorry.' He moved closer, putting his arm around her, and Charlotte leaned in. 'That must have been appalling.'

She nodded. 'I still miss her.'

After a few moments he said, 'Without your mother, there was no one to protect you.'

Charlotte shook her head. 'I was seventeen. I protected myself.' She sat straighter. 'That was the year he introduced me to the man he wanted me to marry. A man with the right pedigree and business connections that would help him. I was supposed to be especially nice to him, but the guy was like my father. He thought other people existed for his convenience. Including me.'

Alessio's arm tightened. 'He must have got a shock when he realised you wouldn't stand for that.'

She lifted her head, noting the glint in his eyes and the grim set of his jaw. He looked angry. On her behalf.

Her throat closed. At seventeen she'd been out of her depth and terrified when her would-be fiancé tried to force her into sex.

What wouldn't she have given for Alessio by her side then? But she'd managed alone.

Charlotte stifled the realisation she didn't want to manage alone any longer. That knowledge threw her, making her blurt out more than she'd intended.

'It wasn't pleasant, but I managed. I ended up with a badly torn dress and bruises to my wrists, but he needed to have his nose reset. Needless to say, the business deal didn't go through.' She paused. 'That's why I never dated. I...'

'You don't need to explain, Charlotte.' He lifted her hand and pressed a kiss to her knuckles that softened every tense muscle. 'I'm sorry you had to defend yourself in that way. I'm sorry your own father caused so much pain.'

He paused, his expression full of an emotion she couldn't read. 'You are a remarkable woman, a strong and valiant woman. One I'm proud to know.'

Strong? She'd always tried to be. But now her feelings for Alessio had grown far deeper than sexual attraction.

Looking into his eyes, she feared she might not be strong enough to cope with leaving him.

CHAPTER THIRTEEN

CHARLOTTE WALKED DOWN the cobbled street, barely taking in her picturesque surroundings. Not because she'd grown too accustomed to the quaint lakeside town, but because her world had just slipped off its axis.

She blinked against the bright sunlight, pausing outside a shop that sold beautifully wrapped nougat and boxes of almond biscotti. In the window she saw her reflection. Wearing a blue summer dress and with her hair down, she looked like any carefree tourist.

Except she was anything but carefree.

Days ago she'd recognised her feelings for Alessio had deepened into love. That had scared and thrilled her, for she'd had no expectation of and precious little experience of love. And while Alessio was clearly capable of deep love and loyalty, she knew she couldn't take Antonia's place in his affections.

Alessio had been at pains to ensure Charlotte understood he could offer only sex. She'd gone into the affair with her eyes open.

Except he'd unwittingly given her far more than sex. His passion, respect, tenderness, even the challenges he set her, had given her something unexpected. A belief in her own value. Confirmation of what she'd told herself for years but never completely believed. She'd spent too long listening to her father's putdowns, then feeling cheapened by the appalling situation that last year at home.

Alessio made her feel strong, proud and sexy. A woman who had the right to demand whatever she wanted from the world, or a lover.

Charlotte drew a shuddery breath as tingles of excitement and anxiety rippled through her.

There was only one lover she wanted, and he was already spoken for.

He was in love with his dead wife.

No matter what she wanted from him, there could be no future with Alessio. Or could there?

She turned and started walking. Her boat to the island was due to leave soon.

But she wasn't ready to return. She felt numb, her brain whizzing in too many directions at once. She needed time away from the island, away from Alessio, to think and decide what to do, because her life had changed irrevocably. Whenever she was with him, it was too tempting to believe in happy-ever-afters instead of cold, hard reality.

She'd talk to the boatman and negotiate a later ride back.

Slipping on her sunglasses, she stepped into the piazza, surrounded on three sides by shops and restaurants and on the fourth by the lake. Instinctively she paused, taking in the gorgeous scene, the holidaymakers in bright colours milling around under the trees, the outdoor tables filling and the sun glinting off the water. And across the water L'Isola del Drago.

How she'd miss it. Miss *him*.

'Charlotte.'

She turned and there he was, as if her troubled thoughts conjured him. Something snagged in her chest, and it took a moment to catch her breath.

How could that be when mere hours ago they'd made love until they were exhausted? She should be growing immune to his spectacular looks.

It's not his looks. It's him. The whole flawed, fascinating, wonderful man you've fallen in love with.

He strode towards her with that deceptively lazy gait and heads turned. Women stared and stood taller, straightening their clothes and hair. Some locals hailed him and he returned their salutes. But he didn't stop until he reached her.

His slowly unfurling smile made her jittery stomach settle, and for a moment her worries fled as she basked in his attention.

'What are you doing here?' She'd never known Alessio to leave the island. His great-aunt had hinted he hadn't left it since his wife's death. 'Is something wrong?'

He shook his head. 'Everything is fine…now I've found you.'

Charlotte felt winded. By his unexpected presence and the implication that things hadn't been fine until he'd found her. Was she misreading him? Her thoughts were so jumbled and her emotions so chaotic she didn't know what to think. Today's news had already unsettled her.

'I'm piloting your boat back to the island,' he said.

'You? But you don't come here!'

One black eyebrow rose lazily. 'Yet here I am.'

But Charlotte was aware, even if Alessio wasn't, of the way staff in the surrounding restaurants whispered and stared. No matter what Alessio said, his presence here was noteworthy.

If there wasn't some emergency, surely it was a positive thing that he'd left the island? Like it was positive that he spent more time with the other is-landers instead of living like a total recluse as he'd seemed to earlier.

'*Why* did you come, Alessio? I thought you had meetings.'

He shrugged and looked towards the gleaming speedboat at the end of the pier. It wasn't the boat she'd arrived in, and she guessed it was his pri-vate vessel.

'It was time for a break from work.'

He held out his arm but didn't meet her eyes.

Because he knew she'd find that hard to believe? This was the man who lived for his work. It was only in the last few weeks he'd begun keeping any-thing like normal business hours. Now they spent every evening together as well as the nights and increasingly long siestas.

'Shall we go, or would you like me to buy you a coffee or a gelato first?'

'Nothing, thank you.'

Her stomach had been churning with nerves all morning, and she didn't want to test it with coffee. She slipped her hand through his arm and let him lead her towards the boat.

The idea that he was here because he'd missed her sent delight dancing through her. Could it be as simple as that? As simple and profound?

He'd changed so much from the surly recluse she'd first met. She knew he enjoyed being with her, not just for sex. Now they knew each other as friends as well as lovers since they talked about anything and everything.

Except his marriage. Other than explaining about Antonia's miscarriage, he was still taciturn about that.

That squashed her leaping excitement. Yet as they walked through the sunlit piazza, his tall frame brushing close, she couldn't help wondering if his following her off the island was significant.

Her heart missed a beat as she thought about why she'd come here. He couldn't know about her earlier appointment.

Which meant she'd have to tell him. She swallowed hard and leaned closer to his comforting warmth, revelling in it while she could.

Everything was about to change, and she had a premonition it wasn't going to be easy.

Alessio matched his stride to Charlotte's, nodding to acquaintances but not stopping to talk. Another time. For now he needed to leave. Not because coming to the town for the first time in years was difficult. On the contrary, it had been remarkably easy.

No, what made his skin prickle as if it were too tight to contain him was the need to be alone with Charlotte.

All morning he'd been restless. Sheer determination had seen him through the first of several online meetings. But he kept thinking of Charlotte, wondering what she was doing, wishing he could be with her.

The castello *was empty without her.*

That realisation had brought him up short. The place was his haven, even if it held awful memories. But today, for the first time, he needed to get away.

To Charlotte.

He tightened his hold and slanted a glance at her. With her gilded hair loose over her shoulders and her breasts budding against that pretty blue dress, she looked fresh and irresistible.

Something lurched in his gut. The knowledge that he shouldn't have initiated this affair. He was too tainted for a woman like her.

Yet how could he resist?

Part of him he didn't recognise had taken over today. A reckless, fun-loving Alessio that reminded him of the man he'd been before marriage and disaster.

He guided Charlotte onto the boat, saw her settled, and cast off. Minutes later, throttle in his hand, the boat leapt to life beneath his touch. The way his heart leapt when she touched him.

'Where are we going?' Because the boat wasn't headed towards the island.

'You haven't eaten lunch yet, have you?'

She shook her head and Alessio felt his mouth curve in a tight smile. Tight because his growing need for her, the fact that he'd had to interrupt his day because he missed her, rang warning bells he'd deliberately ignored.

'Good. I raided the larder and have a picnic packed.' His smile became a grin as he saw her eyes widen. 'Don't worry. It's all delicious. I have an excellent housekeeper.'

Her mouth curled primly. 'So I hear. I have it on good authority that you're lucky to have her.'

Alessio laughed, the sound torn away as he pushed the throttle and they sped along the lake. The sun shone brightly and the wind was fresh on his face, while beside him Charlotte looked flushed and happy.

Life was good.

Even if just for this day, life was good.

It was a revelation, a benediction, and Alessio thanked whatever fates had led Charlotte to him.

A short time later, he pulled in to a private pier. Once the boat was secured, he grabbed the picnic blanket and basket and helped Charlotte ashore. She was nimble enough to get ashore herself, but he liked how her hand turned in his, accepting his help, then stayed there, as if she too needed the physical connection.

'Who lives here?' she asked.

Alessio looked up at the pale pink three-storey villa as they walked through the rambling garden. 'Nobody at the moment. I own it, and a cousin lived here until recently. I'll look for a tenant soon, but for now it's empty.' He turned to Charlotte. 'We're totally alone.'

Dancing blue eyes met his, and heat shafted through him. '*Totally* alone?'

'Absolutely.' His voice was gravel and heat as that ever-present need for her surged anew. He saw it reflected in her face, felt it in her hand squeezing his.

Something passed between them. An understanding, an urgency. An unspoken primal message that had him dropping the picnic basket and drawing her into the deep shade of a spreading chestnut tree.

'Charlotte.' He tossed the picnic blanket down, but spreading it out would mean relinquishing his hold on her. Instead he backed her up against the tree trunk. 'I want you, Charlotte. Now.'

Such simple words, yet they revealed a devastating truth. Alessio had wanted her from the moment he'd seen her, dripping wet, emerging from his lake. He hadn't stopped wanting her since. If anything, his need had grown and grown until it was all-encompassing. He couldn't imagine life without her once she'd gone to Venice and her stellar career. If he had to, he'd—

Her hand on his cheek brought him back to the present. To eyes that held the same mix of desperation and anxiety that he felt. Was it possible Charlotte felt the same?

His tense shoulders eased as if a weight had been removed, and something unfamiliar fluttered in his belly. Hope. It had been so long, he almost didn't recognise it.

'I want you too, Alessio.' Her hands were already busy at his shirt buttons, spreading the fabric wide so she could plant her palms against his heaving chest.

He scrabbled in his back pocket for a condom as her nimble fingers undid his trousers.

'I love your efficiency,' he murmured as he sheathed himself.

Her laugh was a throaty gurgle that went straight to his groin. 'I love how aroused you are,' she countered. 'So strong and virile and—'

Charlotte gasped as he lifted her off the ground

and pinioned her with his body against the tree. She grabbed his shoulders and with his help, put her legs around his hips. Alessio was rigid with anticipation and delight. How could he ever get enough of this woman?

He delved between her legs, tugging aside lacey fabric to be sure she was ready. Her slick folds and convulsive shudder at his caress gave him the confirmation he sought. No time now for foreplay. He *needed* her urgently.

'Charlotte…' Her name was a sigh of delight as he pushed in slowly, watching her pleasure as he settled at the heart of her. *'La mia ragazza d'oro.'* His golden girl.

'Alessio.'

She held his gaze with eyes so bright they scorched him to the soul. When she took his hand and planted it on her breast, he couldn't wait any longer.

He swallowed to clear his throat enough to apologise because he couldn't do slow and thorough, not now. Not with her gazing up at him with such yearning. Except her sweet body moved against his. His throat closed, and words failed him as he tumbled into abandon.

The union of their bodies, and he could have sworn, their souls, was perfect. They moved in sync, every thrust and twist perfection in that ancient dance that had never felt so right. The tension built with each touch, each slide, each gasp.

She was with him all the way, drawing him deeper, making her own demands to match his.

Thunder roared in his ears as his climax exploded. He felt Charlotte jerk and clench, her fingers digging deep into muscle as she arched her head back and rode the same seismic waves of pleasure as he.

Had he ever known anything so superb?

They clung together, and Alessio was glad for the tree at her back to prop them up when it seemed nothing but instinct kept him upright.

How long it took for his mind to re-enter his body, he had no idea. As for lowering them both to the ground and the discarded blanket, he had no real memory of it. He just found himself lying, with Charlotte clasped tight in his arms, as they rode the aftershocks.

The sun had shifted by the time they roused enough to do up their clothes and think about food.

'I owe you a button,' he murmured as he watched her sit up and straighten her dress. A row of small buttons ran down the front of the bodice, and one was missing, creating a tiny gap that tantalised him with its glimpse of creamy flesh. He'd tugged the buttons undone, needing to fondle her bare breasts, and in the process had torn one free.

Charlotte slanted him a look that pretended to admonish but was all satisfied woman. 'I should set you to find it in this grass. You'd be here for hours.'

'Maybe you could help me.' He shifted closer,

following the line of buttons with his index finger. 'We work better together.'

He saw her expression shift, an arrested look in her eyes, before she turned away. 'Maybe we should eat first.'

It wasn't Charlotte's desire for food that caught his attention but the indefinable difference in her voice.

Alessio's instinct sounded a warning. Something had changed. Her incandescent brightness had dimmed, and she was putting distance between them.

He leaned across, covering her hand with his. 'Something's wrong.'

It wasn't a question. It was a certainty, confirmed when she didn't immediately deny it but kept her attention fixed on the picnic basket. Except Alessio sensed she wasn't seeing the wicker box.

Where were her thoughts? What was it that made her jaw tense and her brow furrow?

He didn't even stop to question his need to understand and help. She was more than a casual sexual partner. She was important, special in ways that he couldn't articulate.

'Charlotte.'

Slowly she turned, and he read anxiety in the glitter of her overbright eyes. 'I went to the doctor this morning.'

Alessio's heart dipped and shuddered. His fingers tightened into a vicelike grip as he fought rising fear. In the past he'd heard the worst from a doctor. It took every atom of control not to panic and assume the worst now.

He fought to keep his voice even. 'What's wrong? Are you sick?'

How sick? Pain hemmed him in, pressing down on his chest and shearing through his gut.

'I'm okay. I'm not sick.'

Alessio stared, watching her mouth move, hearing her assurance but taking extra time to digest that. He swallowed, his throat thick. 'But there's something.'

She nodded, the movement jerky. 'There is.' She took a deep breath and that tiny gap in her bodice stretched wider. 'I missed my period. I'm pregnant.'

CHAPTER FOURTEEN

ALESSIO'S FACE TURNED sickly pale. His hard yet comforting grip on her hand ended when he dropped it as if it burned.

There was silence as his gaze raked her. Silence but for the thunder of her pulse and the hiss of his indrawn breath.

Not happy about the news, then.

What had she expected? Brilliant smiles, talk of shared parenting and a future together?

Charlotte hadn't been that foolish. But nor had she expected the look of complete horror that made his flesh shrink back against his bones, emphasising the harsh austerity of his features.

'Pregnant.'

It wasn't a question, yet she sensed he couldn't quite believe it. She didn't blame him. She'd been astounded when her regular-as-clockwork period failed to materialise. Even more when the doctor this morning had confirmed her suspicion. Charlotte had put her faith in the protection Alessio always used, even knowing it wasn't one hundred percent effective.

Trust her to be that point-something-percent exception!

'Yes.' She cradled her fingers in her other hand, but it wasn't the same as *his* touch. 'I'm pregnant with your child.'

The words turned him to stone. She couldn't even see his chest rise or a pulse flicker. And somehow, in that instant of total stillness, Alessio seemed to draw in upon himself so that now he resembled not the lover who had taken her to bliss but the forbidding stranger who hadn't wanted her in his home. As if their weeks of intimacy had never happened.

Except they had. There was proof of it as tiny dividing cells in her womb.

Charlotte took a sustaining breath, still grappling with her own shock and mixed emotions. She hadn't planned on a baby and didn't feel remotely ready. Yet at the same time, beneath the anxiety and uncertainty lurked excitement at the idea of having Alessio's child.

Apart from the fact that she loved him, she recognised a yearning to have someone to care for and love. If she couldn't have Alessio, and his expression indicated that was unlikely, she could have a child of her own. It struck her how terribly she missed the warmth of her mother's love.

Instinctively she wrapped her arms around her middle in a gesture that made Alessio's eyes widen. He shot to his feet, muttered an apology and strode away so fast on those long legs he almost ran.

Charlotte stared, unprepared for such a reaction. Surprise, yes. Even anger. But not this.

Yet you knew he'd already lost a child. And a beloved wife. You should have understood this would open up all sorts of memories for him.

Charlotte hunched in on herself, watching as Alessio stalked the length of the garden to the lake, to stand staring out at his island home. Every inch of his tall frame looked tense, from his wide-planted feet to the high set of his shoulders and the grim cast of his profile.

It was impossible to believe this was the man who a short time ago had lost himself in ecstasy with her, so driven by need that he'd taken her up against a tree, fully clothed and desperate for release.

Now he looked like a man who wished he was anywhere but here.

Charlotte wilted as if her spine slowly melted. She'd gone into this affair with her eyes open, yet when she discovered herself pregnant, she'd harboured the tiniest hope that this would bring them together even more.

As if a baby would make Alessio love you.

She winced at the scoffing voice in her head. It was too like her father's. Like the brutal voice of her would-be fiancé, hurling abuse as she ran from him, clutching her torn bodice after he'd tried to rape her.

Desperately she tried to gather her composure. She should be used to facing life's challenges alone. If she had to do that now, so be it.

She was busy fending off anxiety when a sound made her look up. Alessio stood before her, hands deep in his trouser pockets, his face blank of emotion except for the troubled knot on his brow.

'I beg your pardon, Charlotte.' His deep voice sounded clipped and unfamiliar. 'That was not well-done of me. I apologise.'

She cleared her throat. 'It's a shock for us both.' She didn't want him thinking she'd planned this. 'I'd never thought of getting pregnant. I'd assumed condoms would be enough.'

'I understand.' His mouth lifted at one corner in a mirthless smile. 'I should have known better, since this happened once before.' He dragged in a breath so deep his chest heaved. 'I'm sorry for not protecting you better. I should have thought to suggest backup contraception, but—' his smile turned wry '—I was too busy enjoying myself to think.'

That wasn't what she'd expected. 'It's as much my responsibility is yours.'

She might have been a virgin, but she had a responsibility to take care of her own body. Why hadn't she sought extra protection? Surely it couldn't be because she'd wanted… No, that was impossible.

Alessio sank to the ground nearby. Not close enough to touch, Charlotte noticed with a sinking heart. He might accept joint responsibility for the pregnancy, but keeping his distance didn't bode well. Not for her or the baby.

'There are things I need to explain.' His voice was gentle, his expression stark. She understood, as if she hadn't before, that she wasn't going to like what he had to say.

* * *

'Go on.'

Alessio watched her push her shoulders back as if preparing for bad news. Her chin angled up and her gaze was clear, yet her arms were still wrapped protectively around her middle. It almost killed him to think of how badly he was about to let her down. His gut grabbed painfully. Because he'd be yet another man, after her father and her fiancé, who'd abused her trust.

The realisation made his tongue stick to the roof of his mouth.

He wanted to be the man she wanted.

A man she could rely on to be there for her and her child. He felt torn in two by that need and the knowledge he could never be that, no matter how much he wished it.

His mouth was full of the dull tang of failure. The sharp ache of regret pierced his chest, and his cramped lungs struggled to draw in enough breath to fuel his words. But he owed Charlotte the truth. Even if it made her hate him more than she was already beginning to.

'You know Antonia and I married because I accidentally got her pregnant.'

He watched Charlotte's mouth turn down at his choice of words. To her this was a unique event. For him it was history repeating itself. He shuddered as cold enveloped him.

'We'd been friends for years, so at least we had

that to build on when we married. Like me, she was an only child, but unlike me, she had no relatives. I became her only family. She relied on me.'

Alessio felt his throat tighten and paused. 'We were living in Rome but came here soon after the wedding.' Charlotte had said it was a good place to raise a child. But that's not why they'd moved. 'She wanted to live quietly, away from the paparazzi and the gossipy social scene. She didn't want people seeing her.'

'I'm not surprised. It must be hard having the press snapping photos of you all the time.'

'There was more to it than that.' He felt like there was a boulder lodged in his chest. He hadn't spoken about this with anyone. 'On a routine medical check, the doctor noticed something wrong and sent her for tests.'

Alessio remembered in minute detail hearing her news. Their lives had transformed from that moment.

'Antonia was diagnosed with a terminal illness.' He heard Charlotte's gasp and made himself continue. 'She could have had treatment that might have lengthened her life, but she chose not to because she wanted, more than anything, for our baby to have a chance to survive. She was playing a waiting game, hoping and praying she'd live long enough for that.'

There was a rustle of fabric as Charlotte moved towards him. Then, as his eyes met hers, she sank back where she was. He couldn't cope with anyone's touch right now. He teetered on a knife-edge of self-control.

'Oh, Alessio! I'm so sorry.'

He nodded. 'It wasn't that she minded the world seeing photos of her pregnant. It was that she didn't want everyone to see her waste away. She was a proud woman, vivacious and glamorous, and she couldn't bear the world to see that change. She didn't want sympathy or attention. She needed privacy. As time went by, she cut off ties with friends, relying more and more on me.' As if he'd been able to give her what she needed! 'I promised to look after her and the baby. To do everything possible to protect them.'

He'd promised, but he'd failed abysmally.

'How appalling for her, and how incredibly difficult for you.'

Alessio's head jerked up again to meet Charlotte's sympathetic stare. He wanted to bask in it, take every good thing she offered, all the warmth and tenderness, the understanding and generosity of spirit, and hold them close. But he didn't deserve that.

'The doctors believed there was a hope for the baby. In fact, things went so well that I went to Rome overnight on business.' He paused, remembering. 'That night she miscarried.'

There was nothing he could have done, they'd said. Nothing anyone could have done. But he knew, and he knew Antonia knew too, that if he'd been at home, she might have rested more, letting him look after her as he always did, soothing her fears and reading to her in the evening until she fell asleep.

Gentle fingers touched his and he wanted, so badly, to turn his hand to hold Charlotte's, clinging to her as if she could eradicate the dark maw of guilt.

Instead he slipped his hand away.

It was time to end this. 'After that, Antonia gave up, and I watched her waste away before my eyes, mentally even more than physically. It was hell. Then suddenly she seemed to rouse. She looked almost like her old self, with a determination I hadn't seen in ages. She talked of reconnecting with friends and making the most of the time she had left. I'd been asked to visit an estate to advise on an auction of rare heirlooms, but I'd refused. Antonia urged me to go, said I needed a break from her and the *castello*.'

He looked away, unable to hold Charlotte's eyes. 'She waited until I'd left. Then she somehow found the strength to walk out into the lake and drown herself. She'd planned it all along.'

He heard Charlotte's muffled sound of distress, but wisely, this time she didn't reach for him. He couldn't blame her.

'The only thing I could do was manage the public narrative to make it seem like a swimming accident. I owed her that much.'

Especially as he'd failed her and the baby. He'd sworn to protect her, but he hadn't been able to stop her descent into depression and suicide.

'You poor man.'

He caught Charlotte's troubled gaze. 'Poor Antonia, don't you mean? I promised I'd look after her. I should have suspected—'

'How could you have known that's what she planned? You said yourself she seemed better, talking about connecting with friends.' She leaned in, her expression earnest. 'You did your best to care for her, Alessio. And at least she had the solace of knowing you loved her.'

He jerked back then, and found himself on his feet, towering over Charlotte. His voice, when it came, was harsh. 'But I didn't. I cared for her as a friend, a good friend. I tried to be a decent husband, but I never loved her or she me. Maybe if I had…'

Alessio shook his head and turned away, his gaze turning inevitably to the island that was his beloved home and at the same time, his prison.

He turned back to Charlotte, drinking in her gentle beauty and, even now, her sympathy. As if his revelations hadn't proved how undeserving he was.

'I know the situation's different now. *You're* different. But I can't go there again.' His throat closed convulsively. 'I can't be a father and husband. I can't be the man you and the baby deserve. I'll support you both. Anything you need, you can count on from me, and I won't interfere with any decisions you make about the child. But that's all I can offer. Nothing more.'

CHAPTER FIFTEEN

CHARLOTTE SLEPT ALONE that night for the first time since the ball when Alessio had swept her into his arms, carried her up to his bed and taken her to heaven.

It seemed a lifetime ago.

She stared at herself in the mirror, seeing the evidence of a sleepless night. But there was some small comfort in pulling on familiar work clothes. For years her work uniform had been a concealment, useful when she wanted to keep her distance, especially from men.

She shrugged into a jacket, feeling the need for extra armour in case she saw Alessio at breakfast. But instead of wearing her usual navy or black, today she'd chosen her one colourful outfit. The dark crimson lent colour to her cheeks and made her tired eyes sparkle. Or maybe that was anger at the way he'd cut himself off from her so completely.

They'd talked on the way back to the *castello* yesterday, and later. Rather, she'd talked and Alessio had politely listened. But it was like addressing a brick wall. Not quite that bad, for he'd nodded from time to time, acknowledging her words. But nothing she'd said had made any difference.

She blinked fiercely as her eyes prickled, and

she concentrated on yanking her hair up into a businesslike bun.

She'd considered leaving it down around her shoulders, knowing Alessio liked it that way. But this wasn't a problem to be solved by using her femininity or trying to seduce him.

She grimaced. If anything, *she'd* be the one seduced, for even furious and hurt by his rejection, she was still weak as water around him.

To her shame, she'd spent the night missing his lean strength. Not even for sex but for the comfort of being held close and that sense of blissful intimacy where it felt everything was right in the world.

Alessio was the most stubborn man she'd ever known to believe himself responsible for two tragic deaths when it was clear to any impartial observer that neither had been his fault. Antonia had planned her suicide carefully, getting him out of the way so he couldn't stop her.

But his guilt showed him to be a man who cared deeply and who took his responsibilities to heart, even if he hadn't loved Antonia.

Guiltily Charlotte recalled how her heart had jumped at that news. As if that meant he was free to love her.

She spun away from the mirror, unable to meet her haunted eyes.

He doesn't love you and never will.

He made that clear from the start. He spelled out the rules for a short-term affair.

A baby won't change his feelings, no matter how hard you wish it.

Charlotte breathed deep, trying to find at least an appearance of calm. She should be used to it by now—being alone. Being unloved. But today it felt harder than ever to face a new day.

The scent of coffee reached her as she paused in the kitchen doorway. She frowned, pulse quickening as she saw the man busy at the counter, squeezing fresh orange juice into a glass.

He looked up, dark eyes locking on hers, and Charlotte felt that familiar tremble of longing. To hide it, she smoothed her hands down her straight skirt and entered.

'What are you—?'

'Getting you breakfast. You work too hard, and I want to be sure you have a decent breakfast instead of waiting on me.' He paused, and what he said next stole her breath in a great whoosh of air. 'You have to think about the baby.'

The baby you don't want.

The words hovered on her tongue.

But *she* wanted it. The more time passed, the surer she became. Charlotte had no illusions that being a single parent would be easy, even with Alessio's financial support, but she'd manage. She always managed.

She walked to the table, her legs only a little wobbly, and took a seat.

'What if there *is* no baby? There's always termination.'

Alessio's olive skin blanched, turning his face the same sickly shade as when she'd told him she was pregnant. He couldn't bear the thought of being a father, but it seemed nor could he bear the idea of ending the pregnancy.

'That's what you're thinking of?' His tone was sharp.

Charlotte thought of letting him believe so, but despite how much she hurt, she couldn't torture him that way. 'No. I'm not.'

She found it telling that Alessio hadn't suggested that option. Many men would have.

Alessio set the glass of juice in front of her. 'Or there's milk. I wasn't sure if you'd want coffee.'

'Juice is fine.'

He didn't meet her eyes but busied himself at the kitchen counter as if he found this as difficult as she did.

'We need to talk, Alessio.'

'I know.' He swung around, carrying a plate of pastries and a bowl of thick yoghurt topped with fresh berries. 'There are things to sort out, arrangements to be made. But later. For now, concentrate on your breakfast. Would you like an egg?'

Charlotte blinked up at him. Eggs, dairy foods and fresh fruit. Had he been researching dietary needs for pregnant women? Did he intend to supervise all her meals for the remaining weeks she was in the *castello* to be sure she looked after herself?

She didn't think she could bear that parody of a caring partner, solicitous and excited about her pregnancy.

'Actually, I'm not very hungry. I'll eat later.'

'Charlotte, you need to—'

'Don't tell me what I need to do, Alessio. You're in no position to give orders unless it's about my job.'

Her chair scraped as she shoved it back and stumbled to her feet. She felt queasy, but surely it was too soon for morning sickness. No, what made her nauseous was this situation. A man she loved who would never return her feelings. A decent man whose instinct was to care but who was so caught up in grief and self-blame that she feared he'd never be free of his past.

Charlotte's hand curled around the back of the chair. 'Tell me this, Alessio. If our baby is a boy, he'll be the next Conte, won't he?'

Slowly Alessio nodded, his expression grave.

'How will he ever be able to take up the role if you have nothing to do with him? I've seen for myself that the title is the least part of being the Conte Dal Lago. It's about taking a lead in the region and supporting people. That's not something you pick up overnight.'

Alessio shrugged. 'I had to learn for myself. My

father was too busy enjoying a life of luxury else-where to worry about his commitments here. But I wouldn't do that to my...' He paused. 'If the child is a boy, when he's old enough, I'll make sure he learns what he needs to know.'

Charlotte looked at Alessio's set face, the deter-mined angle of his jaw and those broad shoulders that carried so many burdens. He was so resolute that she felt the last of her hopes tumble and crash. It didn't matter what she said or did. She wouldn't change his mind.

'It's all about duty with you, isn't it? You mar-ried out of duty. You tried to be the perfect hus-band because it was your duty. Now, when the very mention of a new baby makes you turn green with nausea, you're determined to do your duty, to en-sure there's someone else to carry on your respon-sibilities when you're gone.'

She couldn't look at him anymore. The pain was too great, clamping her lungs so she could barely breathe, making her heart ache as if it bled. She turned to the window, where she could see a glo-rious sunny day beginning.

'Let's leave that discussion about the arrange-ments you want to make. I can't face it today. I've had enough of your concern and your duty.'

Charlotte spun away and walked to the door, conscious all the time of Alessio's gaze heavy be-tween her shoulder blades. She waited for him to speak, to acknowledge the truth of what she'd said.

Or even protest she was wrong about his feelings for her and their unborn child.

But he said nothing. His silence enveloped her like a chill cloak, dousing the heat in her cheeks and frosting her heart.

She'd lost. There was no argument she could make that would reach him. Nothing she could do to make him love her.

Midnight had struck. The Cinderella fantasy which had crept into hopeful life was dead.

Alessio stood at his office window, staring sightlessly at the view.

Instead of the lake, in his mind's eye he saw Charlotte, her mouth crumpled with hurt while her eyes blazed with desperate determination. Charlotte walking out on him, her shoulders stiff and head high while he'd wanted to do anything, say anything, to make her turn back to him. To have her walk into his arms, smile up at him, lay her head against his chest and lean close.

His heart thudded a ponderous beat as he relived the effort it had taken not to relent but to watch her walk away.

Because walking away was best for her and the child, no matter how much he yearned for the light she'd brought into his life.

She didn't understand how his failure with Antonia had stained his soul, marked him as a man who couldn't be trusted to protect those he cared for. He knew all the logical arguments about it not being his fault. Beatrice had berated him with those more than once, and he was no fool. He understood what she said. Yet in his heart, in his dark soul, the guilt remained.

He couldn't, wouldn't taint Charlotte with that darkness. He couldn't risk failing her and her unborn child.

At the same time, he couldn't sustain the current situation. For days, Charlotte had avoided him. He'd let her, rather than force his presence on her, because he'd seen her confusion and hurt. That only reinforced the knowledge that he did the right thing, keeping his distance.

Nevertheless, they needed to talk. There were arrangements to be made for her care during pregnancy. For the child.

A great ache opened up inside him like a yawning chasm at the thought of her alone and pregnant somewhere far from him. He wanted to be with her so badly. Because he was selfish. He craved—

Sounds on the pier interrupted his thoughts. He looked down and recognised Mario loading his boat for a trip across the lake. He carried a big basket aboard, baked goods for a nearby market. But then he loaded a large suitcase.

Alessio frowned. Mario hadn't mentioned a trip. He was pondering that when another figure emerged. A slender woman with hair the colour of old gold.

Charlotte. Alessio stiffened. She climbed onto the boat and took a seat near the suitcase.

His heart stopped beating, and the bright morning light faded towards darkness. When he remembered to breathe, he found himself clutching the window frame, hauling air into cramped lungs.

Something like panic rose inside him, a great wave of dread. Charlotte was leaving like he wanted. But too soon, far too soon. He wasn't ready.

Deliberately he tightened his grip on the window, forcing his feet to stay planted where they were. This was best. It wasn't ideal. He'd rather have sorted out the practicalities of his support for her first. But that could be remedied. All he had to do was stay here and let her do the sensible thing.

Alessio blinked, his gaze blurring, as Mario started the engine and Charlotte left him.

They were halfway to the shore, Mario chatting over the putter of his engine, when a roaring made Charlotte turn. She frowned. Was that…?

'The Conte's in a hurry.' Mario watched the speedboat approach.

Charlotte turned to stare at the town ahead of them. She didn't want to talk to Alessio, especially in front of someone else. Her emotions were too close to the surface, and she felt scraped raw.

But instead of passing them, the faster boat slowed. Alessio called out and Mario answered, conversing in the local dialect she couldn't understand. Then the other boat surged away, and she felt stupidly lct down.

Because Alessio hadn't addressed her?

She shook her head at her neediness. The sooner she left and started a new life the better.

Thoughts turning inward, she paid no attention to her surroundings until the boat bumped gently against a pier and Mario offered her a hand to disembark.

'No thanks. I'm fine. Can I help you with the basket?'

A deep voice came from above. 'Mario isn't getting off here.' She looked up and there was Alessio, his windblown hair and darkened jaw making him look more like a pirate than ever. Or maybe it was the hard glitter in his narrowed eyes as he reached down to take her hand.

Startled, Charlotte looked beyond him. They weren't at the town but at the villa they'd visited together days before. In the distance she saw the spreading tree where they'd made love, where she'd told him about the baby and he'd explained why he could never be part of her life.

Instinctively she pulled back, but Alessio was too quick. 'We don't want an audience for this, Charlotte,' he whispered in her ear. Then more loudly he added, 'Mario doesn't want to be late for the market.'

Charlotte opened her mouth to say she had her

own plans for the day, but she was already letting him lead her up off the boat. Where was her willpower? She feared this weakness she couldn't control.

He led her away from the water, not even dropping her hand when the engine revved behind them and Mario left.

Sunlight kissed her bare arms and his fingers encircling hers were hot, yet Charlotte shivered, cold to the bone.

'What do you want, Alessio?' Her voice was harsh, rough with emotions she didn't dare identify.

He stopped and turned towards her, the morning light behind him. 'You're leaving. Without even telling me!'

'I—'

'How could you do that?'

Charlotte stood taller. 'Do what? Go? That's what you want. You're the one pushing me away. The one who can't bear to think about, much less see our child.'

He shook his head. 'But to leave without a word.'

'We've said everything that matters. Besides, I—'

'No, we haven't.' Alessio shifted, and now she could read his expression. What she saw startled her. He didn't look angry but haunted, desperate even. His nostrils flared and his broad chest rose as if he struggled to drag in enough oxygen. 'I need to explain.'

'No more explanations! I understand your feelings.' She tugged, trying to slip out of his grasp.

'That's just it. You don't.'

For a long moment, his glittering eyes held hers. Then abruptly he let her hand go. Instantly she cradled it in her other hand, missing his touch.

She should march away rather than prolong the agony of being with him, but she couldn't. 'What don't I understand?'

'I want you, Charlotte. I don't want to give you up, or our child.'

The shock waves from his words thundered through her, making her weak at the knees. 'That doesn't make sense.'

Alessio's laugh was harsh. 'I'm not surprised. I'm an emotional mess, not the logical man I used to be. Since you arrived on the island, I haven't been able to think straight. I haven't been able to resist temptation. Haven't been able to sleep, except with you in my arms.'

His voice hit that gravelly note she knew from lovemaking, and some of her hard-fought resistance melted.

Charlotte struggled to be sensible though every instinct urged her to hug him close, since he made it sound like he suffered the same tortures she did. She feared that would resolve nothing and simply ignite the sexual attraction still burning between them.

'Tell me, then. Explain what's going on.' She folded her arms rather than reach for him.

'I said I wanted you to leave and bring up our baby somewhere else. I believed it as I said it, but it wasn't the truth.' He nodded at her shocked gasp. 'I told you that because I thought it better, both for you and the child, to be far from me. My track record is…abysmal. I had one role in my marriage, to protect, and I failed. I couldn't bear to fail you or our baby.'

Charlotte didn't recall deciding to move, but now she was in his space, gripping his shirt front, tilting her head up to hold his gaze.

'You might be a brilliant businessman, Alessio, but in some things you have absolutely no idea. The only way you could fail me, fail us, is to turn your back, the way you have the last few days.'

Strong arms wrapped around her back, pulling her up against his hard body. Heat seeped into her, and it felt like the first time she'd been warm in days.

'I wasn't turning my back. I was hiding.' He grimaced. 'I told myself I needed to give you space, but really I was too scared to see you in case I blurted out the truth.' He drew another deep breath, his chest pushing against her. 'I was even afraid to give a name to my feelings, until I saw you leaving.'

'It's not—'

'Shh.' He put his finger on her lips, his expression gentle, his mouth curling up in a wry smile. 'Let me finish, please.' Yet he paused before continuing as if he found the words hard. 'I saw you get into Mario's boat, and something broke inside me. That's amazing in itself, because not so long ago I thought everything inside me was completely broken. Until you made me see differently. You made me wonder if there could be good things in life again. You made me hope even though I tried to resist. You made me love.'

Charlotte blinked, telling herself she'd misheard. But it was too late. Already her blood effervesced in excitement. 'Alessio?'

'I've never been in love. I never saw it modelled by my parents or felt any love from them. I didn't recognise it. I told myself it was lust, and fun, and companionship. Gratitude even, because you shone a light where in the past there's only been darkness.' His mouth twisted. 'What you saw in me, I have no idea. I've been a grumpy, difficult b—'

This time it was Charlotte's hand that covered his mouth. She shivered as he pressed a kiss to her palm, and she felt it right to the core of her being.

'You were in a bad place, but *you* weren't bad,' she assured him. 'Your bark was worse than your bite—'

'Most of the time.'

'And there were reasons you found it hard having someone new your home.'

'The main one being that you interrupted my attempt to wallow in self-pity. You kept appearing, demanding things, expecting me to act and get involved, tempting me as no woman has ever tempted me before.'

Sizzling green eyes held hers, and fire crackled in the air between them.

'I mean it, Charlotte. I've never felt like this about any woman. Never *loved* before.' His mouth turned down. 'That only added to my guilt. I'd married Antonia and promised to protect her, but I'd never *loved* her.'

'Oh, Alessio.' Her heart felt so full she thought she might burst. 'You can't blame yourself for that. You two married for the good of your child. You tried your best.'

'I know, I know. But what I feel for you makes me realise how little I really had to give Antonia. I was her carer and her friend but that's all.'

'I'm glad you were her friend. She needed that. But it sounds like she wasn't in love with you either.' She paused, knowing she didn't have the right words, if there were any. 'You both did the best you could in extraordinarily difficult circumstances. You did all you could, Alessio.'

He said nothing, but his expression wasn't nearly as bleak as it had been earlier. Maybe one day he'd believe that.

Finally she couldn't hold back any longer. 'You really love me? It doesn't seem real.'

'I truly do. Which is why I'm hoping you'll give me another chance. For the baby's sake, if not mine.'

'What about for my sake?' Charlotte paused, fighting her learned instinct to keep her feelings to herself. 'I'm in love with you, Alessio.'

His eyes widened, and he lifted her right off her feet, drawing her up till her face was level with his.

'Say that again.' His voice was husky as if he couldn't believe it.

'I love you.'

She watched her words sink in. The stark lines around his mouth somehow lessened, and the furrows on his forehead disappeared. He looked younger, lighter. Happier.

'I haven't even apologised yet. I need to grovel at your feet for the way I've behaved.'

Charlotte shook her head. 'You can kneel at my feet anytime you like, but there are other things you could be doing there apart from grovelling.' She saw the familiar, hungry glint in his eyes that softened the muscles at the apex of her thighs.

The blaze of joy in his face and the wicked gleam in his eyes spoke of a man ready to turn his face towards the future, even if it wouldn't always be easy.

A great weight lifted off her heart. This really was happening!

'Can we take it as read that you're sorry and I'm sorry too?'

'You've got nothing to apologise for, Charlotte.'

'Apart from wrecking your peace and making you face lots of things that have been painful for you.'

She'd seen how deeply his guilt ran over the past. Ever since he'd explained what had happened to his wife, Charlotte had been horrified at how much he'd had to endure, and how she'd inadvertently dredged up so much pain.

But she couldn't regret anything when Alessio smiled at her like that. Slowly, oh, so slowly, he lowered her to her feet, and the delicious friction between them felt like a promise.

'I have a confession to make,' she murmured. His eyebrows rose. 'I wasn't leaving today. Mario was just giving me a lift to the market.'

'But the suitcase?'

'His great-nephew's. He left yesterday with a friend who didn't have room in his car for a suitcase. Mario is taking it ashore to send on after him.'

Alessio shook his head, his expression brimming with laughter. 'I've never run so fast as when I saw you leaving with that case. I told myself I was doing the right thing, staying there, but I only lasted thirty seconds. I swear my feet didn't hit the stairs going down the tower.'

'I'm glad you came after me, even if it was a mistake.'

He shook his head. 'It was no mistake, Charlotte. It was the best, most sensible thing I've done in my life. I intend to stick close, woo you and persuade you to stay with me, always.' On the last word, his voice dropped to a resonant note she felt deep in her heart.

'You want me to live with you in the *castello*?'

'I want you to live with me wherever you like. Here or in Rome or…'

'I like it here.' Suddenly she felt shy. Because of the way Alessio watched her, as if she were utterly precious.

'I want to make you my *contessa* if you'll have me. I know I have a lot of ground to make up, and you may not want to marry—'

'I can't think of anything I'd like more. And *not* for the sake of our baby. I'm being totally selfish.'

'Excellent.' His smile was that devastating one, guaranteed to melt her bones. Just as well he was holding her tight. 'Because I am too. I want to marry you because you make me happy, Charlotte, happier than I've ever been.'

His head swooped low, his mouth covering hers reverently as if sealing a lifetime's promise.

Charlotte kissed him back with her whole heart.

It wasn't long before she was grateful he'd had the foresight to lead her deep into the garden. For what came next was utterly joyous and just for the two of them.

EPILOGUE

ALESSIO SMILED AS he looked into the cosy room. 'I thought I'd find you here. Aren't you coming downstairs to help welcome the guests?'

Beatrice lifted one imperious eyebrow. 'Stop bothering an old lady. I'll be down in my own good time. You and Charlotte are perfectly capable of managing without me. The recent *castello* balls have been a huge success.'

He smiled, surveying the real reason his great-aunt was taking her time. The dark-haired toddler almost asleep in his bed, one hand clutching his teddy bear, the other resting on the picture book the old lady held.

The bond between little Luca and his great-great-aunt was an unexpected joy. And it kept Beatrice so busy she had less time for poking her nose into Alessio's affairs.

'Very well, we'll expect you soon. Remember the Swedish ambassador is coming early and wants to talk with you. And Luca's babysitter is waiting.'

'If the ambassador's coming early, what are you doing here? Shouldn't you be downstairs supporting your wife? Marrying her was the best thing you ever did, but you can't afford to take her for granted. She's turned you and this place around completely, and you need to support her.' Beatrice paused. 'It's months since you took Charlotte to that beach resort at Langkawi. You should plan another trip soon. Maybe to Switzerland since she loves it so much.'

Alessio repressed a smile. Beatrice just had to give advice. And it had been she who'd asked him to call her in good time before the guests arrived. 'Yes, Aunt Beatrice. I couldn't agree more.'

'Oh, you…' Beatrice narrowed her gaze. When he was a child, that beetling look might have made him nervous. Now Alessio read her silent laughter. 'Begone with you. Go to your wife, immediately!'

Chuckling, he headed a few metres down the hall. Pushing open the door, he halted, stunned. When he'd left their bedroom, Charlotte had still been wearing a wrap, putting on her make-up.

Now she stole his breath.

'La mia ragazza d'oro,' he murmured when he found his voice. 'You look more and more beautiful every day.'

In a dusky pink strapless gown, its full-length skirt sprinkled with what looked like thousands of diamonds, Charlotte rivalled any fairy-tale princess.

Alessio wrapped his arm around her waist and planted a kiss at the base of her neck so she gasped and clung to him. The subtle scents of vanilla, cinnamon and fragrant female hit his sense receptors and hardened his body.

'Alessio.' Her welcome never grew old. Nor did the shimmering delight in her smiling eyes when he lifted his head. 'You look more and more handsome. Sometimes I can't believe this is all real.'

'Believe it, Charlotte.' His voice deepened as emotion rose. 'All I am I owe to you. I've never been so content and fulfilled.'

She beamed, her eyes so bright they rivalled the brilliance of the ruby and antique pearl earrings he'd given her to match her heirloom pendant.

'You know,' he murmured as he kissed her, 'I don't think I ever told you the end of the family legend.'

'About the baron who claimed the virgin who'd been left for the lake monster?'

'That's the one.' Alessio traced the soft flesh at the edge of her bodice, unable to resist torturing them both with what they couldn't yet have. 'Tradition has it that they were supremely happy, loyal and loving. And while most of my forebears were greedy, grasping types, every generation or so, one of them fell for a blue-eyed, golden-haired virgin, and his fate was sealed. His destiny lay with hers.'

'You're joking!'

'It's true. I didn't tell you before we were married because I didn't believe it myself. Now I know it's true. I love you with all my soul, Charlotte, and always will.'

'That's just as well.' The emotion in her eyes belied her faux brisk tone. 'Because I'll love you forever, my darling Conte.'

Neither moved for long moments, lost in their

good fortune. Then Alessio thought of the arriving guests. Regretfully he ushered her out towards the grand staircase. 'I'd much rather spend the evening alone with you.'

'We only have to wait a few hours.' Yet her voice told him she felt the same. 'Did you see Beatrice? I thought perhaps we should tell her our news.'

Charlotte's hand pressed to her abdomen in a gesture as old as time, and Alessio felt that familiar surge of protectiveness. He lifted her hand and pressed a kiss to her knuckles, holding her close.

How had he ever thought to survive without Charlotte and the family they were making?

'You know Beatrice. She'll fuss over you and try to give orders. Let's keep it our secret a little longer.'

'I like the sound of that.' For a second longer they shared the moment. Then Charlotte sighed. 'The ambassador's coming early. We'd better go.'

'Practicality as well as passion. No wonder I love you with all my heart.'

Tenderly, proudly, Alessio led her down the stairs.

This woman had given him back his heart and given him a future as well. What more could he ever want?

* * * * *